Family
Recipe

Family Recipe

WITHDRAWN

Coco Simon

Simon Spotlight

New York   London   Toronto   Sydney   New Delhi

This book is a work of fiction. Any references to historical events, real people, or real places are used fictitiously. Other names, characters, places, and events are products of the author's imagination, and any resemblance to actual events or places or persons, living or dead, is entirely coincidental.

SIMON SPOTLIGHT
An imprint of Simon & Schuster Children's Publishing Division
1230 Avenue of the Americas, New York, New York 10020
This Simon Spotlight hardcover edition May 2020
Copyright © 2020 by Simon & Schuster, Inc.
All rights reserved, including the right of reproduction in whole or in part in any form.
SIMON SPOTLIGHT and colophon are registered trademarks of Simon & Schuster, Inc.
Text by Valerie Dobrow
For information about special discounts for bulk purchases, please contact Simon & Schuster Special Sales at 1-866-506-1949 or business@simonandschuster.com.
Designed by Ciara Gay
The text of this book was set in Bembo Std.
Manufactured in the United States of America 0520 LSC
10 9 8 7 6 5 4 3 2 1
ISBN 978-1-5344-6540-4 (hc)
ISBN 978-1-5344-6542-8 (pbk)
ISBN 978-1-5344-6541-1 (eBook)
Library of Congress Catalog Card Number 2020932457

Chapter One
Family and Friends

I threw down my bag, then picked it up again and stuffed it into the cubbies that Dad had built us by the back door.

My sister Kelsey yelped, "Heeeeyyyy!" behind me when the door slammed before she got inside.

"Too slow!" I said, and walked into the kitchen, kicking off my shoes.

"Too messy!" said Dad, pointing to my shoes. "In the cubby, please."

"Molly slammed the door on me," Kelsey whined behind me.

"Welcome home, girls!" said Dad. "It's nice to see you, too!"

Dad had made us a platter of cheese and crackers

and set it out on the kitchen counter. Kelsey and I dove for it hungrily.

"Did you eat lunch?" Dad said.

"Yeah," I said, stuffing a cracker and cheese in my mouth. "But that was, like, three hours ago."

"I miss snack time at school," said Kelsey.

"Kelsey, we haven't had snack time at school since kindergarten!" I said.

"Well, they should have it in middle school," said Kelsey. "Everyone would be less cranky in the afternoon." She gave me an accusing look as she ate a cube of cheese.

"I'm not cranky," I said after I swallowed another mouthful of cheese and crackers. "I'm hungry."

"Okay," said Dad. "Eat your snack then let's see. . . ." He walked over to the bulletin board in the kitchen, where Mom kept all the calendars and schedules. "Today is Tuesday. Molly, you have soccer at four thirty."

"Yep," I said, picking out two crackers and a bit of cheese before making myself a mini sandwich. "I know."

"So that means homework needs to get started pronto," said Dad.

"Yep," I said again while devouring my mini sandwich. "I know."

"Kelsey, I need you to help Mom with dinner when she gets home from work," said Dad, still examining the bulletin board. "Wait, wait, you have hockey. Now how is this going to work . . . ?"

"Dad," said Kelsey, finishing off the last of the good crackers. "Mom went over it this morning. Jenna is driving me to hockey and you are taking Molly to soccer."

"Right!" said Dad, smacking his head. "I thought Jenna was working today, but she's just tutoring after school."

I went back to my cubby and took out my laptop and my French book.

"What are you doing?" asked Kelsey.

"Starting my homework," I said, setting up at the table.

"Now?" asked Kelsey suspiciously.

"I have soccer in an hour and a half," I said. "And hours of homework tonight, which is totally insane."

"You could start it when you get home from soccer," Kelsey said.

I rolled my eyes.

Kelsey is not entirely organized. My dad says Kelsey likes her downtime, but in reality, she just doesn't like to do homework.

It's not that I like doing homework, but I honestly don't mind when it's interesting. The drill stuff, like my French homework, is really annoying, so I like to just bang it out when I get home and get it over with.

Kelsey would be whining about her Spanish homework at nine o'clock tonight.

"Kelsey, why don't you take a page from Molly and get started too?" asked Dad.

She sighed dramatically.

Dad sighed dramatically back at her.

"How are we even related?" I grumbled, and grabbed another cube of cheese.

"You have Mom's systematic approach," said Dad. "It's good that at least half the family has it."

I laughed. "More than half," I said.

Mom and I are organized, and Jenna is too. Dad says that he and Kelsey, on the other hand, are "dreamers."

"Okay, now Mom and dinner," said Dad, looking a little worried. "I was going to prep some veggies so she can make an egg dish, but . . ."

"Mom and eggs," I reminded him, "are generally not a good pair."

"Definitely not," said Kelsey. "Remember when she tried to hard-boil them?"

Both of us started giggling.

Even though Mom's family owns a restaurant, she cannot cook to save her life. She tried to hard-boil eggs to make egg salad once, and we still don't know what she did, but all the eggs started exploding. It was a huge mess. I'm pretty sure there's still some egg stuck on the ceiling over the stove.

My theory is that Mom senses us, especially when we talk about her. Just at that moment, the phone rang, and sure enough, it was her.

Kelsey spoke to her first, going on and on about how ridiculous it was that she had so much homework.

I knew exactly what Mom was saying to her without even hearing it. *If you stopped complaining and just did the homework, you'd be halfway done by now.*

Mom and I are a lot alike in that way. I have no time for drama or complaining.

Kelsey handed me the phone.

"Hi, honey," said Mom. "How was your day?"

"Fine," I said.

"Fine?" asked Mom, and I could tell she was wrinkling her face up.

"Yeah," I said. "You know it takes a few weeks to get into the swing of things with a new school year."

"That's true," said Mom. "Do you have a lot of homework?"

"While Kelsey was complaining, I got half of it done," I said, smirking as Kelsey stuck her tongue out at me.

Mom laughed. "You're just like me, kiddo!"

After I was done talking to Mom, I handed the phone to Dad.

He talked to her for a few minutes and then said excitedly, "Hey, girls, Grandpa made his famous chili at the restaurant today! Mom's bringing it home!"

"Dinner!" Kelsey yelled, punching the air.

"Yeah!" I yelled too.

Grandpa's chili was super delicious, so I was already looking forward to it even though my stomach was full of cheese and crackers. But I'd be hungry again after running around during soccer practice.

Dad smiled and nodded. He hung up and said, "Dinner is saved."

Family Recipe

I knocked off most of my homework pretty quickly after that and went upstairs to get ready for soccer.

I started playing soccer when I was in kindergarten, and I've loved it ever since. I love how fast the game is, but I also love that there's a strategy. It looks like a crowd of people is just running around after a ball, but in reality, you have to have a plan to get the ball down the field. Everyone on the team has a specific role for moving the ball around.

I heard my older sister Jenna burst in the front door downstairs, because Jenna doesn't do anything quietly.

"I'm hooome!" she called.

"Start the parade!" Dad says like he always does.

Jenna is in high school, and she can drive, which she thinks makes her a lot cooler than she is, but she actually is pretty cool.

She is also kind of intense. Mom says that Jenna is a "demon on the court" in tennis, which makes sense because Jenna is really competitive.

"Molly, ten-minute warning!" Dad called upstairs. "Soccer starts in twenty, and it takes ten to get there!"

I threw my hair in a ponytail and headed

downstairs. I didn't love having practice after school because I was already tired. We had it in the mornings the week before school started, which was better, even though I had to streak myself beforehand with tons of sunscreen, making my eyes all stingy when I sweated.

"Hi, Molls," said Jenna, slamming the fridge. "Dad, what do we have for a snack? I'm starving."

Dad pushed the cheese and cracker plate toward her, and Jenna scowled.

"They ate all the good crackers!"

"There are bad crackers?" Dad said. "Huh. I didn't realize we could divide crackers into good and bad. That's good to know."

"Dad, you know what I mean!" Jenna fumed and opened the cabinet to rummage through it. She opened a box and stuffed a few crackers into her mouth.

"Eat some cheese and fruit with those," said Dad. "That's the healthy part."

"Dad, I'm old enough to drive a car," said Jenna. "I know what healthy food is!"

Dad sighed and gave Jenna a hug. "You may be driving, but I will always see you as the adorable toddler who called herself Wenna because she couldn't say her *J*s yet."

I burst out laughing as Jenna rolled her eyes at him. Dad is so sentimental sometimes that we call him Mr. Goo.

"And *you*," said Dad dramatically, hugging me hard. "You were my baby who refused to say Dada or Daddy. That's the first word most kids say! But not you. It was Mama, Mama, Mama. Then Wenna. Then dog . . ."

I was laughing because I knew the rest. "Then 'kit cat' for Henry the cat," I said.

"Yes!" said Dad. "Kit cat, *then* Daddy. Finally! You nearly killed me!"

I smiled. We actually have a video of me sitting on Dad's lap right before I touched his nose and said "Daddy" for the first time. He was so happy he looked like he was going to cry.

"Sorry about that," I said, then hoisted my soccer bag over my shoulder.

"Okay. My child who now loves me has soccer," Dad said to Jenna. "Kelsey is . . . where is Kelsey? Kelsey?" he bellowed upstairs. "Are you on the phone before you finished your homework?"

"Probably," said Jenna, smirking.

Kelsey came downstairs looking guilty. "I had to ask Lindsay what the assignment was," she said.

"Kelsey . . . ," Dad warned.

"Fine, I'll start my homework."

"Great!" said Dad. "Jenna will take you to hockey while I take Molly to soccer. Okay, kiddo," he said to me, and we headed out to the car.

Even though I've been sitting in the front for a long time now, it still feels weird to ride next to Dad in the front seat.

"You excited about the game this weekend?" Dad asked.

"Yeah," I said, "but the first game of the season is always hard. There are some different girls playing this year."

"That's expected," Dad said. "That's why you have practice, to get to know each other's strengths and rhythms."

"Yeah," I said, and rested my head against the window.

One of the good things about Dad is that he understands that even though I like to talk, I also like to be quiet at times. Jenna talks nonstop and Kelsey is either talking or texting, and we can all be a little noisy, but sometimes I like to zone out, especially when I'm getting ready for soccer. It kind of clears my head so I can focus. Mom used to joke that I had an on/off switch and nothing in between.

Dad pulled into the lot at the soccer field and we got out of the car.

I guess it's kind of weird that Dad still comes to my practices now that I'm in middle school. I noticed the other day that most kids get dropped off, but Dad sits in the bleachers, watching. He's not one of those parents who yells from the sidelines, which I am very thankful for, but he definitely pays attention.

"Okay," he said, taking his coffee mug. "I'll be in the stands if you need me, honey. Have a great practice!"

I waved and trotted off to the sidelines.

My BFF, Madeline, was on my team. And this year, Riley and Isabella were playing with us too, which was both good and weird. Good because I liked them both, but weird because Riley was better friends with Kelsey than me.

Coach Wendy had us out on the field before I could think about it too much. We warmed up and did some drills, and then she had us count off for a few three-on-three scrimmages. I liked those because if you have a full team on the field, you aren't always on the ball. When it's just the three of you, it can be much more intense.

Madeline was on my squad. We've been best friends since preschool, and we've been playing together forever, so I know almost without thinking which way she's going on the field or when she'll decide to take a shot.

We were passing the ball back and forth pretty well when Riley said, "Hey, guys, I'm on your side," which startled me a little.

I nodded and passed to her, and she tripped over the ball. Her face got red, and she said, "Sorry," and looked down at the ground.

Riley is a good player, but when she thinks people are watching or there's a clutch moment, she sometimes just whiffs on the ball.

"It's okay," I said. "Let's work you in better."

I nodded toward Madeline and she nodded back.

"Play forward," I said to Madeline.

I passed the ball up the field to her, and she made a really nice kick to Riley, who sank it in the goal.

"Now that's it!" called Coach Wendy happily. "That's it, that's it, girls! I saw what you did there. Worked each other in and figured out how to play together. Great job!"

Riley took a bow, and I laughed. I looked up at Dad, who gave me a thumbs-up and a grin.

We played for another thirty minutes before Coach Wendy blew the whistle.

"Girls," she said. "This weekend is our first game. I don't care if we win."

Everyone looked at each other.

"I care that you play well as a team," Coach Wendy explained. "We have a long season and plenty of games to win, but let's do this as a team, okay?"

We all nodded.

"Now give me a G!"

"G!" we all yelled.

"What's that for?"

"Go!" we yelled.

"G is for?" she said, smiling.

"Great!" we yelled.

"G is for?"

"Goal!" we yelled. "Go! Great! Goal!"

I wondered if I was the only one to realize that

the cheer didn't exactly make sense, but it sure got us all riled up.

Once I sank into the seat in the car, I realized how tired I was. "Oof," I said. "That knocked me out."

"Well, you did a heck of a lot of running," said Dad.

"Speaking of running, did you get a chance to run today?" I asked him.

Usually he went in the morning, but once school started, it was harder for him to get out in time.

"Nah, I missed today," Dad said, wincing. "And I definitely feel it."

"There's a track around the soccer field," I said, thinking about it. "When you bring me to practice, you can just do some laps instead of sitting in the bleachers."

"What, you don't like your old dad sitting around watching you?" he joked.

"Dad," I said, already knowing where this was going. "I like having you at practice. I want you to be at practice. But I also know how much you like to run."

Dad smiled. "Ah, okay. I thought you were trying to nicely tell me you were too old to have your dad with you! I thought maybe I embarrassed you."

"I know," I said, and rolled my eyes. "Mr. Goo, you are very sensitive!"

Dad laughed. "You know what Mr. Goo who is sensitive wants?"

"What?" I asked as we turned onto our street.

"Some chili!" he said. He pointed to our car, which was in front of us.

"Then step on it, sir," I said. "Because if we don't get home soon, the rest of the family is going to eat it all! Follow that chili!"

"Give me a *C*!" said Dad.

"*C*!" I said.

"Wait, we don't have time to spell out chili," said Dad. "How about just 'go'?"

"You know, maybe we should say, 'Give me a *G*' for Grandpa," I said, picking up my bag. "Go, Grandpa, for saving us from Mom's dinner!"

Dad cracked up and said, "Let's keep that cheer between us."

Chapter Two
The Assignment

Every morning in school, we meet in the cafeteria until the morning meeting, which is usually a bunch of announcements, is over. Then we go off to our first class.

Soccer the day before must have wiped me out more than I thought, because I was feeling kind of hazy. I bumped into my cousin Lindsay as I headed toward my first-period class, which was history.

"Are you still asleep?" she joked. "You usually get up so early!"

"I know!" I said. "I'm wiped out from school and soccer."

"Are you working after school?" she asked.

I nodded. "Yep. I have a shift today."

Family Recipe

Our grandparents own a restaurant in town called the Park View Table. They run the whole thing, and it's seriously a family operation.

Mom works there in the accounting office. Uncle Mike, who is my mom's brother and Lindsay's dad, runs Donut Dreams, the donut counter in the restaurant. Mom's other brother, Uncle Charlie is in charge of all the inventory and orders.

Jenna and my other cousins Rich and Lily also have shifts at the Park after school and on weekends. This year, Lindsay, Kelsey, and I started working at the Park too.

Lindsay and Kelsey manage the Donut Dreams counter, while I'm a runner, which means you "run the floor." So if my sister Jenna, who is a waitress, serves someone a hamburger and they ask for ketchup with it, I would be the one who runs to get the ketchup and brings it to the table. I also bring more napkins and refill customers' water glasses, that kind of thing.

It's not very glamorous, but to be honest, there's nothing really glamorous about working at a restaurant. It's a lot of hard work.

"Me too," Lindsay said. "Ugh, being a runner seems like a very un-fun job."

"Nah," I said. "I don't mind it. Actually, your job at the counter seems worse. If there are no donut customers, it must be *sooo* boring!"

"But when it's slow, we can just stand around and hang out!" said Lindsay. "I guess Grandpa and Nans gave us the right jobs."

We slid into our seats. Lindsay's seat was in front of me, while Eric Sellers had the seat behind me.

Ms. Blueski was our history teacher and she was new, which was a little odd, since we don't get a whole lot of new people who move to our town.

She had just finished her student teaching, and we were her first class of kids, which Eric decided to take advantage of. He was usually pretty annoying, but he's been even more obnoxious lately. I knew he was just testing Ms. Blueski.

"Can I go to the bathroom?" Eric asked.

I turned to see him waving his hand. I had just seen him come out of the restroom before class, so I knew he was trying to get out for a few minutes to waste some class time.

"I am sure you *can* go to the bathroom, Eric," said Ms. Blueski, and the whole class giggled. "But you *may* go to the bathroom after I get to a break in the lesson. You just came from morning meeting and you had a break between classes."

Eric looked mad and wiggled around in his seat uncontrollably. "But I really have to go!" he said.

Ms. Blueski looked at him. "Do you think you're going to wet your pants?" she asked. "Because if so, then please do go now."

The class was howling with laughter. "Look out! Eric is going to wet his pants!" called out Adam Linzer, who was sitting on my right side.

Harry Watson scooted his chair away. "Hey, don't get me wet too!" he called.

Eric turned red.

"Eric, why don't you go now?" said Ms. Blueski. "We will get started so the rest of the class doesn't have to wait for you, but I can wait to talk about the assignment until you get back."

Eric hurried outside.

"Run, Eric!" yelled Adam. "Before you have an accident!"

"Okay, okay," said Ms. Blueski. "Let's settle down."

Three minutes later, Eric came back in. He must have just been standing in the hall.

"All right," said Ms. Blueski. "Now this is a history

class. History is important because we learn about the future from things that happened in the past. It gives us an understanding about the world and a context for how we live now. You may think history has to do with wars or things that happened a very long time ago, but history can be more recent, too. And it can be personal. Every one of you, for instance, has a history."

We all thought about that for a second. Most people in this class were born in Bellgrove, Missouri. We've spent our whole lives here, and most of us could recite our own history, which was kind of boring.

"Our first assignment is going to explore the History of You," said Ms. Blueski. "And to start off that exercise, we're going to do a family tree. I have one up here as an example on the whiteboard.

"You'll need to fill in as much of the tree as possible with parents, grandparents, aunts, uncles, and cousins, going as far back and as far out as you can. To get you started, I have some blank trees that I'm passing around."

I took a sheet and turned to pass one to Eric.

"We're going to start off with the basics you know," said Ms. Blueski. "This week's assignment is to talk to your family to see how much of the tree you can fill in with the spots I provided. I think when you do this, you'll find out all sorts of interesting things about your relatives that you may not know as you gather as much information as you can."

Everyone looked down at their sheet. It seemed kind of straightforward. I put down my name first, then Jenna's and Kelsey's.

Eric leaned forward and said into my ear, "Is that your real tree?"

"What?" I said.

"Since, you know, you're adopted," Eric said.

"Oh my goodness!" I said. "I had no idea!"

Adam laughed. Lindsay turned around and said, "So are you writing your family history or Molly's family history, Eric?"

"I'm just saying that she might write her mom down on her tree, but that's not her real mom," said Eric.

I felt my heart start to beat fast.

Everyone I grew up with knew I was adopted. I mean, I don't look at all like my family. My skin is a different color, my hair is kind of different, and my eyes and nose look different too. But nobody outside my family and close friends really talked about it. It was just a fact: "Molly is adopted."

Sometimes people said or did weird things, like the time I went to my friend Ava Baker's house for dinner, and Mrs. Baker made me wonton soup. I guess she thought that because I was born in South Korea, I would like it, but I didn't. And wonton soup is Chinese, not Korean.

Mom said that one of the things about being adopted is that you might have to educate people like Mrs. Baker.

I didn't feel like educating Eric just then.

"Have you ever met your mom?" asked Eric. "I mean, your *real* mom."

"I've seen her real mom," said Lindsay. "She is actually my aunt Melissa. Aunt Melissa is pretty real."

I looked at her gratefully.

"Well, yeah, I mean she's Molly's mom, but if she does her history on a tree, there's got to be her other family," said Eric. "Like she has a mom and a mother."

My other family? My stomach was flip-flopping around.

"She has one family," Lindsay said firmly. "Although maybe you have another family. Maybe your real mother is a monster ghoul, because only a monster ghoul could produce such a jerk."

"His mom can be really strict," Adam said, laughing again.

"Hey, back off my mother!" said Eric.

"Is there a problem over there?" asked Ms. Blueski.

"We're gathering information," Adam told her. "About Eric's monster mom."

The class laughed.

Then the bell rang, and I was never so happy to be able to run out of a class.

Chapter Three
Dad Is My Real Dad

I went to French class, and then lunch. Dad packed our lunch every day, so I didn't have to waste time in line. I flopped down at the table with Madeline.

"Bad day?" Madeline asked.

"Yeah," I said, sighing.

"What happened?" Madeline asked.

"Eric Sellers can really be a giant jerk," I said.

"Can be?" Madeline said. "You mean he is. Anyway, what did he do?"

"He's just a jerk," I said. "I don't even want to talk about it."

"So who is going to help me with this coding assignment?" moaned Madeline.

I shrugged. Today I had enough problems of my

own to solve. I didn't really have time for Madeline's.

After lunch I passed Lindsay in the hall on my way to phys ed.

"Hey!" she said, grabbing my arm. "Are you okay?"

"Eric is just a jerk, that's all," I said. "I'm good."

"He sure is," Lindsay said, nodding. "Don't let him get to you."

"He didn't," I said. I smiled to reassure her, but as I headed toward the locker room, I knew I was lying.

Luckily, in phys ed we just had to run on the track. Sometimes I run with Mom and Dad on the weekends, when they do shorter distances.

The thing I love about running is that I can just let my mind go. And when I'm running for myself, not, say, as part of a relay team, I only have to think about my pace, my legs moving, and my arms pumping. I don't have to worry about anyone else but me in my own lane.

Today we were doing sprints. As soon as I heard the whistle I tore down the track as fast as I could. The wind blew my hair around and felt good hitting my face. I wasn't really paying attention until I saw Dad standing at the fence.

He was leaning on it, talking to Mr. Walsh, who was the phys ed teacher. Dad is a carpenter and teaches woodshop at the high school down the street. Mr. Walsh and Dad do a running club together, so sometimes Dad comes down to the track to do a few laps with Mr. Walsh after school.

"I'm not spying!" said Dad as I jogged over.

"He's not!" laughed Mr. Walsh. "I asked him to come down with the forms for the race we're doing next month."

"But," said Dad, "I saw this speeding bullet coming down the track and thought, 'Whooooa!'"

"And he said, 'Hey, that's my girl!'" said Mr. Walsh.

"It sure is!" said Dad, beaming.

I blushed a little. "Okay, Dad. I have one more class left. Do you want to come watch me during English lit, too?"

"I love English lit," said Dad, teasing, "but I left the car at school so Jenna can drive to work, and I'm going to run home now."

I noticed just then that he had changed from his work outfit into his running shorts and T-shirt.

He hoisted his backpack on. "Got all my stuff in here!"

Mr. Walsh blew the whistle. "Okay, crew, bring it on in!"

He gave Dad a high five and said, "Run tall, Chris!"

"Bye, Dad!" I called, then followed Mr. Walsh over to the bench. I watched as Dad ran off.

Dad had what Mom called a long gait, which in running means that you have a wide step or stride. He could take about three strides running and be half a block away from me. But no matter how fast Dad went, his body always seemed really calm and relaxed. It looked like the only thing moving was his legs.

Seeing Dad made me feel better. I mean, he was my *real* dad, no matter what Eric Sellers said.

Chapter Four
Family, Work, and Perfect Pie

After school I waited on the front steps with Kelsey and Lindsay. Nans was picking us up to take us to the Park for our shifts.

Grandpa was always in a better mood when a lot of family members are working shifts in the restaurant together. If there was a shift where no family members were available, he hired local college students to help out but he wasn't happy about it. He loved having family around all the time.

Nans was pretty short and drove this really big white car. You could barely see her head above the steering wheel, so it almost looked like the car was driving itself.

Kelsey opened the car door and called out, "Hiya,

Nans. Here's the crew reporting for duty!" She jumped in the front seat next to Nans while Lindsay and I sat in the back.

"My girls!" said Nans. "I'm so glad to have such a lovely group of girls as my granddaughters!

☀ ☀ ☀ ☀ ☀

When we got to the Park, we changed in the workroom, which was just a little room off the kitchen with lockers and benches and a full length mirror on the wall. There was a rack of uniforms hanging in the corner.

I had to wear a Park collared shirt and a long apron and black pants. Lindsay and Kelsey wore aprons too, but they could wear jeans and Donut Dreams T-shirts, which made me a little jealous.

I went to the mirror to pull my hair back off my face in a wide headband, and I saw Mom come in behind me.

"Hi, girls!" she said, hugging Lindsay and Kelsey. She came over and kissed the top of my head. "Everyone have good days?"

We all nodded. Lindsay looked over at me for a second, but I didn't want to catch her eye.

"Put your hair in a pony, pumpkin," said Mom. "Rules are rules."

I sighed. "Grandpa and his rules," I said.

"Actually, that's not Grandpa's rule. That's a health and safety rule for all places that serve food. I mean, you wouldn't want someone's hair in your food. Oh, that'd be really . . ."

"Totally disgusting," I said, and pulled my hair into a pony, but I kept the headband on too.

We all walked out. I passed Uncle Mike and Uncle Charlie, who were having a meeting with a salesperson at the counter. They waved, and I saw Uncle Mike go give Lindsay a hug hello.

Sometimes I feel bad that I have a mom and a dad, while Lindsay just has her dad. I mean, she has all of us, too, but her mom died a couple years ago. She once told me that it was hardest after school, because that was the time of day when she most realized her mom was really gone.

After she told me, I told Mom. I felt bad about telling Mom something Lindsay had shared only with me, but Mom's been helping Lindsay a lot since her mom passed.

When I told her, Mom got really teary but said

she was glad she knew. "We look out for each other in this family," she said. "So you need to tell me when someone is sad or upset so we can all help. That's what a family does."

Then she talked to Uncle Mike and to Nans, and now, even if Uncle Mike is there, Mom always makes sure either she or Nans is there after school for Lindsay too.

It's not the same, but it's still reminds her there are other people who love her. Mom is really good about figuring out how to make stuff better.

I walked out of the workroom, tying my apron behind me. Jenna was doing setup, which meant she was checking tables before the dinner rush, making sure there were silverware and napkins at each place setting.

"Hey, little sister," she said. "Can you make sure all the salt and pepper are good to go?"

I nodded and headed over to the station where we kept pitchers, condiments, and all the stuff you'd need to go with your meal. I made sure all the salt and pepper shakers were full, which was another one of Grandpa's pet peeves.

"Half a shaker of salt?" he'd say if he spied one

on the table. "Customers are going to think they will only get a half a hamburger, too!"

My older cousin Rich was waiting tables with Jenna, and he came over and pulled my headband.

"Gold star from Grandpa!" he said, teasing. "Hair off your face and a ponytail! But before you get that star, let's check. Maybe you left out a grain of salt in that shaker."

"Well then, that one is going to your table!" I said, laughing.

He grinned and grabbed the salt shaker and put it on his tray.

There was only one table that had a customer. What was weird was that in just a short time I'd started to know who the regular customers were.

Mrs. Rose, who was a nurse, was always here early. She was still in her scrubs. She was here every day around this time because she stopped after her shift at the hospital.

She was only in her late thirties but sometimes she could look older because she always seemed so exhausted. She was really sweet though.

Jenna nodded to me, so I headed over to Mrs. Rose's table with a pot of coffee.

"Can I fill you up, Mrs. Rose?" I asked.

"Oh yes, sweetie," she said. "I need another cup so I have energy to get to my dog-walking group. Otherwise those puppies will run all over me!"

"I didn't know you did a dog-walking group!" I said excitedly.

"It's for the rescue group I volunteer for," said Mrs. Rose. "We take dogs that don't have homes and care for them until they can be adopted. This way they don't have to stay in shelters. I meet up with the other rescue workers once a week for a dog walk, and we celebrate if a dog is no longer there and has been placed with a family."

"Wait, you can see a dog one week on a walk and the next week the dog is just gone?" I asked, shocked.

Nans is always telling me I have no filter, and I just say what I think without, as she says, *processing it*.

"Well, a rescue home is never meant to be permanent. Sometimes the dogs are with us for a week, sometimes a few months, until we find the right home for them."

I thought about that for a second. "So you might take care of a cute little puppy but then someone else gets to keep it?"

"Yes," said Mrs. Rose. "Sometimes I get attached to the animals, and I miss them when they're gone. Some dogs just make you want to keep them forever. But part of what brings me a lot of happiness is seeing the best, loving homes these animals find for the long term."

I nodded, but I guess I looked a little skeptical.

I saw Grandpa wander over, another pot of coffee in his hand.

"Oh look, Mrs. Rose," he said. "You can tell this is one of my granddaughters, because she's quick on the refill, just like her old granddad!"

Grandpa put his arm around me and grinned. I couldn't tell whether he was checking out my headband.

"You just love having your grandchildren here, don't you?" said Mrs. Rose, smiling.

"Of course I do!" said Grandpa. "I get to see all my grandchildren, and I get to boss them around, like telling them to get over to their station and fill up all those ketchup bottles!"

We all laughed.

I knew Grandpa wasn't totally joking about me getting over to refill the ketchup. He ran a tight ship at the Park, and he was everywhere and saw everything. He liked that I was friendly with the customers, but he also didn't like us to dawdle.

Sometimes I got caught up in conversation with someone and he'd beeline it over to me.

I would say, "Well, Grandpa, I didn't want to be rude," and he would say, "I know, sweetie, but you have to know how to cut off a conversation. They didn't invite you to sit down with them and eat!"

I secretly thought Grandpa and Nans were also worried I would upset someone because I did have that tendency to speak without thinking. It's not like I made people mad a lot, but I did get a lot of eye rolls, with people saying, "Molly, you can't just say that!"

I looked across the restaurant and saw Kelsey wiping down the donut counter. Lindsay was ringing up a kid I recognized from high school and laughing.

The donut counter, Donut Dreams, had a different rhythm than the diner most days. People came in for donuts early in the morning, and then there were two after-school rushes, one after middle school and one after elementary school let out.

Then there was a lull, because not a lot of people

eat donuts before dinner, although in my opinion that would not be a bad habit.

Our shifts were usually from four o'clock to six thirty. If we were really busy, we'd stay until seven. You could feel the restaurant start to change after five o'clock, when the regulars and then families would come in for dinner. It got busier and noisier and people moved faster.

Mom had been trying to convince Grandpa to add a take-out option so people could pick up dinner and eat it at home, but Grandpa wasn't too sure about that.

"Why would you eat food out of a bag?" he would ask. "Here you sit down, someone brings you dinner, and cleans up after you!"

He did have a point.

A few minutes before five o'clock, Nans gave the signal and the waitstaff headed toward the kitchen for a quick meeting.

"Hello, everyone," Nans said. "Let's quickly go over the specials for tonight."

I loved this part, because Nans liked everyone to taste the specials so they'd know what they were describing if anyone had questions.

Tonight, for instance, the special was stuffed peppers with orzo. Nans sliced a few for us so everyone could have a piece.

The peppers were grilled and soft and filled with orzo, which is pasta shaped like rice, and some onions. It was delicious, and I was glad I tried it, because if I had to describe it, I would be able to say that uncooked peppers are crunchy, but once you grill them they are soft and a little sweeter, just like onions.

The other special was a dessert, Nans's famous apple pie. Nans passed out pieces of that too, and she winked as she gave me a really big one.

I smiled because she knew her apple pie was one of my all-time faves.

"Do you need to double-check that you still like this?" Nans asked me.

"I think I do, Nans," I said.

"Since you're the apple pie enthusiast, you're on apple peeling duty," she said.

As everyone else filed out, she put me to work at the counter. She spooned a little bit of the filling into a dish and gave me a spoon.

"I know you just ate a piece of the pie, Molly," she said, "but I want you to taste the filling separately to make sure it's just right. What do you think?"

"Nans, your apple pie is perfect. Like, it just can't get any better. But I wonder if there's a way for us to make apple pie donuts," I said.

"But we have apple cider donuts that everyone loves," said Nans. "I can't make enough of them sometimes."

"I know," I said. "But apple pie donuts would be different, because they would have a filling. Like cream donuts, but instead of cream, the inside could be apple pie filling."

Nans smiled. "Thank you for saying my pie is perfect," she said. "But even perfection can sometimes get better. And let's see what we can come up with for the donuts. While I'm making more perfect pies, it's time for you to hit the floor."

Chapter Five
Curious Kids on My Shift

I gave Nans a quick kiss, then headed out. Kelsey and Lindsay were already getting ready to close the Donut Dreams counter, which annoyed me a little bit because they were almost done with their shift. After they did cleanup and mopped the floor, they'd head to a booth to hang out or eat until my shift was over, and then Mom would drive the three of us home.

"Molls, can you drop the check off at Mrs. Rose's table?" Jenna asked, whisking by me and handing me the paper receipt. "Then I'm gonna need your kid skills with the Sherers." Jenna indicated a table with a mom and three boys, all of whom were crying.

"Oh, boy," I said as Jenna headed over to them.

I love kids, and I'm usually really good with them.

This summer I ran a babysitting group at the lake, which was fun. The parents would drop the kids off with me, but stay on the beach in case I needed help.

I could usually manage four or five at once. I would play games with them or we'd read a book. Sometimes I brought some art projects, but it turned out that anything that involved glue while you were dealing with kids in sand was a very bad and very messy idea.

"Can I get you anything else, Mrs. Rose?" I asked.

Grandpa had taught us to ask that before we gave them the check. "If you just hand them the bill for the meal, the customer will think they can't order anything else. What if they're still hungry? I can't have customers leaving here still hungry!" he had said.

"No, I'm all set," said Mrs. Rose, looking at her watch.

I placed the check on the table. "Please pay up front," I said, exactly like I was taught. "And have fun with the pups tonight!"

"I certainly will," she said. "Are you a dog person, Molly?"

"Yes!" I said, a little loudly, and Mrs. Rose laughed.

"Would you like a dog?" she asked. "Because we

have so many dogs who need loving homes."

"I would just love a dog," I said longingly. "But the problem is Mom and Dad. They think that three kids is enough work, and one dog plus three kids is too much."

"Well," said Mrs. Rose, chuckling, "they have a good point there. Maybe when you're a little older and things settle down, they'll change their minds."

"I hope so," I said, but I wasn't convinced.

"I have to show you the most adorable puppy that came into our group. She's just precious." Mrs. Rose rummaged through her bag and fished out her phone. Then she fumbled for her glasses.

I shifted from foot to foot as I saw Grandpa looking at me and shaking his head from side to side. He gestured toward the table with Mrs. Sherer and her three kids.

Jenna looked a little frazzled. The kids had thrown all the silverware on the floor.

"Here we go," said Mrs. Rose, tapping at her phone. She held it up and I moved in.

"Oh!" I said, and grabbed the phone from her. "Oh my gosh, that has to be the sweetest, cutest, best puppy ever."

I couldn't stop staring at the screen. I wanted to jump inside the phone and grab the dog and run off with her.

She was a tiny puppy with fluffy white fur that almost covered her eyes. She looked like a mini fur ball with two pointy little ears sticking out.

Just then Jenna peered over my shoulder. "Oh, Mrs. Rose," she said. "That's trouble. My sister has wanted a dog forever, and that's a cute one!"

"I know!" said Mrs. Rose. "And this one is just so sweet. And a little sassy, too. She has a way of telling you exactly what she wants."

"Sounds like someone I know," said Jenna, smirking at me. "But right now there's no way Mom will say yes. I do, though, need a little assistance with table fifteen," she said, nudging me.

I sighed and handed the phone back to Mrs. Rose. "Well, keep showing me pictures of that pup," I said. "Maybe one day. But right now I have some fork fishing to do!"

I scooted over to table fifteen, where the Sherers were, and picked up four forks and four spoons. Mrs. Sherer had four knives in front of her.

"Thank you, sweetie," she said. "Here, I can give

you three knives. If we leave them, the kids will try to use them as swords."

I smiled slightly. "Well that's creative," I said.

"Yeah," she said. "They can be quite innovative. Can we get a basket of bread? There was one, but . . ."

"I see it," I said, dropping to one knee. "It must have fallen on the floor."

Mrs. Sherer sighed. "Sorry," she said, looking embarrassed.

"Not a problem," I said. "I'll be right back."

I went to the kitchen to pick up a new bread basket. I sniffed. The kitchen smelled like apple pie.

Grandpa was helping load a tray for Jenna. "Did those Sherer kids go through an entire basket of bread?" he asked.

"No, they dropped an entire basket of bread on the floor," I said.

"Okay, get them another one quick," he said.

I ran back out with the bread, and as I passed Rich, he said, "Hey, can I get refills of water on table ten, please?"

I nodded, dropped off the bread, and grabbed the pitcher.

Table ten was Mr. and Mrs. Grasso, who owned

a bookstore in town called the Book Nook, which I loved.

"Molly!" said Mrs. Grasso. "How lovely to see you. I hope you have time to read between school and work!"

"And soccer," said Mr. Grasso. "I heard you've been tearing up the field!"

I laughed. "Now who told you that?"

"You know your grandfather. We get all the grandchildren updates!" he said.

"Yes, pretty regularly," laughed Mrs. Grasso.

"I need help on eight," whispered Rich as he speed-walked by with a huge tray, heading for the Sherers' table, and I nodded.

"Go, go," said Mr. Grasso. "It's busy tonight!"

"Yep," I said. "Just how I like it!"

I filled their glasses, then hurried over to help Rich unload the tray, setting the plates at each place in the center of the place mat, like Grandpa instructed. You're supposed to turn the plate when you put it on the table so the entree faces the customer, but to be honest, I don't even know what that means.

I looked at the plate of spaghetti and meatballs. Was it upside down? Was there a top to a plate of spaghetti and meatballs? It seemed like a question my math teacher would ask.

The kid was kind of looking at me as I worked it out, so I said, "That spaghetti looks so good. Hope you enjoy it!"

He smiled and dug in. I don't think he cared if it was upside down.

"Fifteen," Jenna hissed as she walked by carrying two plates.

I trotted over to table fifteen, where the Sherer kids had balled up napkins and were throwing them at each other.

"Hey," I said. "Anyone want to have a coloring contest?"

They all looked up. I dug into my apron pocket and took out some packets of crayons that I had loaded up on during setup.

"You can actually use your place mat as a piece of paper," I said, giving each of the Sherer kids a packet of crayons.

I had ripped the packet open for them first, because there's nothing worse than handing a kid a package of something they can't open. I learned that the hard way this summer when I handed out

45

Popsicles that were each sealed in plastic bags.

"Now," I said. "Each of you draw your favorite dessert from the menu. We have ice cream, chocolate chip cookies, or pie tonight." I hoped I was right about the cookies. We usually had three options for dessert on the kids' menu. "Draw which one is your favorite, and if you eat your dinner, you may be able to order what you drew."

I looked over at Mrs. Sherer a little nervously. "Right?" I asked. Some parents were really strict about how many treats their kids had.

"It's a treat to go out to dinner," said Mrs. Sherer. "Or it's supposed to be. So, yes, if you eat your healthy dinner, you can each get a treat."

"YAY!" The kids all started cheering loudly, and everyone in the restaurant looked over.

"Okay, okay," I said. "But let's keep it down a little. Otherwise we'll have to give everyone in the restaurant cookies!"

Just then Jenna shot out of the kitchen, holding a tray on her shoulder. I wanted to try that one day, but she and Rich kept warning me that it was a lot harder than it looked. A dropped tray was the worst disaster for a server because when it crashed to the ground, everyone turned around to stare, and also someone's dinner just bit the dust and the chef had to start over. No one was ever happy about a dropped tray.

I brought a huge stack of napkins to the table. "Just in case!" I said to Mrs. Sherer, who smiled and thanked me.

"Is that good?" I asked six-year-old Christopher Sherer, who was eating his grilled cheese at record speed.

He nodded. "So good!" he said. Then he pointed to the picture he'd drawn of a giant cookie. "And if I eat my grilled cheese, you'll bring me this?"

"Yes, sir," I said, watching him, half-horrified and half-impressed, as he stuffed the rest of the sandwich into his mouth.

"Christopher!" his mother said, exasperated. "Manners count!"

"Okay, should we see if your brothers make the dessert challenge too?" I asked.

"That would be a good idea," said Mrs. Sherer. "Because if only one of them gets a cookie, the rest of the table is going to crumble."

Christopher's two brothers, Bradley and Greg, immediately started drawing their favorite dessert.

But Christopher looked like he was going to cry.

"I have to waaaaait?" he wailed. "But I want my cookie now!"

I peeked around and saw Lily sitting at the host's podium. The host greeted guests, then showed them to their tables and gave out menus. The first rush was over, so she was just hanging out and nobody was waiting.

"Christopher, who's your favorite babysitter?" I asked quickly.

"Lily!" he said.

Lily babysat for the Sherer kids a lot. I have no idea how she did it.

"How would you like to go say hello to Lily while your brothers finish dinner?" I suggested.

"Oh, you don't have to—" began Mrs. Sherer.

"YES!" yelled Christopher, and he climbed out of the booth.

"It's totally fine," I told Mrs. Sherer as I took Christopher's hand and led him toward the podium.

"Christopher!" Lily squealed as he ran to her and gave her a big hug. "You came to visit me!"

"Christopher finished his dinner first and he's patiently waiting for his brothers to finish before he gets dessert," I explained. "He said he wanted to visit his favorite babysitter, Lily."

Christopher was still clinging to Lily. I felt a little jealous. "Even though I was also his babysitter at the lake this summer," I added.

"I'm sure we're both his favorites. Right, Christopher?" asked Lily.

"No," said Christopher. "I like you better."

Lily tried not to laugh. "Oh, Christopher, that's not nice."

"Mom says if it's not nice, then don't say it," said Christopher. "Why was that not nice?"

"It wasn't nice because you don't tell some people you like them better than others," Lily explained.

"Oh," said Christopher, thinking about that.

"Okay, Christopher, I have to help my sister with the table. Stay here with Lily, okay?" I said.

"Who's your sister?" Christopher asked.

"Jenna," I said. "And Kelsey. And Lily is my cousin."

"But you don't look like them!" said Christopher.

I sighed. Suddenly the fact that I was adopted was becoming a big deal everywhere.

"I'm adopted, Christopher," I said.

"Oh," said Christopher. "Do you help your sister with dessert?"

I smiled, grateful that there was no follow-up about being adopted. "I sure do."

"Then you're my favorite sister right now!" said Christopher.

When Jenna and I brought dessert to the Sherer kids, I waved Christopher back over from Lily's station. We put the plates down with a big flourish.

"Ta-da!" I sang. "It's dessert time!"

Mrs. Sherer smiled. "You girls are the best. Thank you so much for your help. We were just talking about making this a ritual for when Mr. Sherer is at the firehouse on Tuesday nights."

I must have looked a little worried, because suddenly Jenna pinched my arm, hard. "That's a tradition we can get on board with, Mrs. Sherer," said Jenna. "We're always happy to see you at the Park."

I nodded and waved at the kids. I looked at the clock on the wall . . . six thirty. Things had really slowed down, so I went over to Grandpa.

"Grandpa, do you need me until seven?" I asked.

He did a scan of the room. "Things look under control here," he said. "Plus your mom, Kelsey, and

Lindsay are all itching to go home, so take off. The old man can pitch in if things get crazy again." He laughed. "Nice job tonight with those kids, honey. You are now going to be assigned to every table with kids. You're a natural!"

"Every table?" I shrieked.

"Hard work is good for you! Melissa," he called to Mom. "I'm discharging Molly. Round those girls up and get them home!"

I noticed he was holding a box. "What's in the box?" I asked.

"Oh! I almost forgot," Grandpa said. "This," he said to me, putting a pie box in my hands, "is from Nans. She said you're helping her make her perfect apple pie more perfect."

"Well, if you insist we taste pie, then we'll just have to eat pie," said Mom. "C'mon, girls. The 'get-out-of-work taxi' is leaving the parking lot!"

"Thank goodness," said Kelsey. "I am *so* tired."

Grandpa rolled his eyes. "Your sister Molly was running all over creation tonight. She's got to be tired, but she isn't complaining!"

"I wasn't complaining," Kelsey said. "I was stating a fact."

She gave Grandpa a hug. Only Kelsey could be sassy with Grandpa without annoying him.

*   *   *   *   *

We trailed Mom out to the car and headed home. When we dropped Lindsay off, Sky came to the door with Nans and waved. Then we drove toward our house, which was on a winding road closer to the lake.

It was still light out at this time of year, although the days were definitely getting shorter. Mom and Kelsey were talking in the front of the car, but I zoned out. The pie was still a little warm on my lap, and I breathed in deeply. The smell made me happy.

It had been a long day, and I still had homework to do. I tried to figure out my strategy. I could bang out my math problems in a half hour. Then I had to write an essay for English lit that might take a while. Then I thought about Ms. Blueski's assignment, and my stomach began to twist a little bit. What was my strategy going to be for that? For the first time in my life, I was going to push one bit of homework off for another night. Tonight was Happy Pie Night.

Chapter Six
No Puppies

Since Dad teaches at the high school, which starts earlier than the middle school, he leaves the house early during the school year. We have Mom to do the morning routine with us and Dad after school. Mom is always on time for everything, so we never really worry about running late. Dad is really laid-back when we get home and doesn't bombard us with questions like Mom does. It's the perfect balance.

Mom was already dressed for work and sipping coffee in the kitchen when I came downstairs the next morning.

"The usual?" she asked, and I nodded, yawning.

My usual was fruit and a bowl of yogurt. I got the yogurt and Mom sliced me some cantaloupe.

"I feel like we're seeing the last of the good melons until next summer," she said. "And I can't believe it's already apple season. Hey, so what did you do to change up Nans's pie recipe?"

"Nothing," I said. "Her pie is delicious as is."

"Well, she seems to think she can make it more perfect," said Mom. "You, my love, must be pretty special to mess with that. And the first apple batch of the season, too!"

Mom is always talking about what seasons certain fruits and vegetables peak, as she says, which means they are best. Despite not being able to cook, Mom is kind of a foodie, and she's always harping about eating fresh fruits and veggies.

Dad built her a really cool vegetable garden one summer, but she killed everything growing in it. I think she worried too much and ended up overwatering the plants every day.

Mom also is in tune with seasonal foods because if a food is "in season"—like, say, watermelon during the summer—when it grows locally, it costs less. As the accountant for the restaurant, Mom cares about things costing less, since they have a really strict budget for how much they can spend on the groceries and food for the restaurant each week. If they splurge on things, or prices go up, they have to adjust the prices on the menu, and people get annoyed if the price of their meal goes up. So you won't see blueberry cake on the menu in February, but you might see pear cake.

Jenna is always saying that when she moves to California, which is her dream, she won't have to worry about that anymore. Fruit is in season all year long there, because it's warm enough to plant and grow crops in all seasons. It sounds really cool to be able to have strawberries in January, but California is pretty far away.

"Kelsey!" Mom called upstairs. "Get going, sweetie! We have to roll in twenty!"

I heard the hair dryer upstairs, which meant Kelsey had not heard a word of what Mom just said. Not that it would matter anyway, since Kelsey did not exactly rush in the morning, no matter how late we were running.

Once Mom made me get into the car to prove to Kelsey that we'd leave without her. A full ten minutes later, when Mom was fuming, Kelsey wandered out of the house, casually peeling a banana, which I guess was appropriate, since Mom went bananas.

Mom checked the calendar and her phone. "Okay, you have soccer after school, so Dad can take you to that. Jenna has a piano lesson, and Kelsey has hockey. Whew, full boat today. Jenna can drop Kelsey at hockey, and then Dad can pick her up and swing back and get you. Are you okay with that?"

I was kind of half listening. "Uh-huh," I said.

"Who's taking me where?" asked Kelsey, strolling into the kitchen.

Mom looked at the clock and sighed. "Jenna will drive you to hockey. And you now have ten minutes to eat your breakfast."

"Okay," said Kelsey, taking out her laptop.

"What are you doing?" I asked.

"Finishing my homework," said Kelsey softly.

"Kelsey Jane!" said Mom. "You didn't finish last night? What were you doing up so late if you weren't doing homework?"

"I wasn't up that late, Mom," said Kelsey. "Besides, my biology homework took forever. I just have to finish some Spanish." She looked over at me.

"I can't help you," I said. "I'm taking French."

She sighed. "Great, you're no help to me."

"Gracias!" I said, grinning. "That means 'thank you' in Spanish."

She glared at me. Kelsey and I mostly get along, but sometimes she really gets under my skin.

"Family helps family," she said. "Isn't that, like, our motto?"

"Yes," said Mom. "It is our motto, it's not 'like' our motto. But everyone does their part. That means you have to do your own homework."

"Mom, can we adopt a dog?" I blurted out. I couldn't stop thinking about that puppy. "Mrs. Rose has the most adorable puppy who really needs a home!"

"No puppies," said Mom, grabbing her keys from the hook by the door. "And clear your plates and wrap up the leftovers, please."

"But why?" I said, rinsing out my bowl before I put it in the dishwasher.

Mom handed us each our lunch bags from the counter. "Don't forget these. And no puppies because they're a lot of work and a lot of responsibility. And with all of us running in five different directions every day, no one is home to give enough attention to a puppy."

"But there are a lot of dogs that stay home all day!" I said as we got into the car. "And Mrs. Rose was at the Park yesterday, and she was telling me that she's in a rescue group for dogs. Do you know what that is?"

"A rescue group?" said Kelsey. "Where do they rescue them from?"

"They take puppies and dogs that are homeless and would go to shelters and they keep them in their houses until they can be adopted. This way the dogs don't have to live in cages in the shelters."

"Poor puppies," said Kelsey.

"Mrs. Rose does great things with those dogs," said Mom. "And it's a lovely thing to be able to take care of them like that. But would you really be okay leaving a young puppy by itself all day, with no one to play with?"

"Well, puppies sleep a lot," I said.

"Not for seven hours," said Mom. "If we leave at eight o'clock and Dad is home at three o'clock, that's a heck of a lot of time to leave a dog alone."

"We could get a dog walker," said Kelsey. "That's what Casey has, because her parents work and are at school all day."

"Sorry, girls, but it's not happening. We're just not

at the point where it's a good situation for the dog or for us," Mom said.

"Okay," I said, pouting a little. "But the next time you see Mrs. Rose, ask if you can see a picture of this puppy. She was the cutest, sweetest thing I've ever seen. Jenna saw the picture too."

"I'm sure Mrs. Rose will help find her a very good home. And now," said Mom, putting on her blinker and pulling into the school parking lot. "I hope you girls have a very good day. I love you!"

"Thanks," said Kelsey, as we walked into school.

"For what?" I asked.

"For distracting Mom so much with the puppy talk that she forgot to ask if I finished my Spanish homework." Kelsey grinned.

I rolled my eyes, and we went to morning meeting.

Ugh, Eric Sellers was the first person we saw when we walked in. "Good morning, ladies!" he said.

I mumbled, "Hi," and Kelsey said cheerily, "Oh, hi, Eric," and kept walking.

"What's wrong?" she asked.

"Nothing," I said. "He's just really annoying."

"He's always annoying, but he's harmless," said Kelsey.

I wasn't so sure. My stomach was doing the flip-flop thing again. Luckily, we didn't have history today.

In middle school we did what they call an A/B schedule, so on A days I had history, French, English lit, and phys ed. On B days I had study hall, math, earth science, and media (my elective this year.)

We went over to our usual tables, and Kelsey gave me a slight wave as she left to go sit with her friends. I usually sat with Madeline at a separate table.

"Give me a G!" said Madeline, giving me a hug. "Aren't you so excited for the game this weekend?"

"To be honest, I haven't really thought about it," I said.

"You haven't?" she asked, shocked. "And here I was thinking you already had a strategy to win it in the second half!"

I laughed. "Well, you won't know the full strategy until we see the team we're dealing with, right?"

"True," said Madeline. "The first game is always hard because you're getting to know your team and the others."

"That's what I was telling Dad!" I said.

"Yeah, Grayson said the same thing." Grayson was

Madeline's older brother. He played soccer for the high school team.

Principal Clarke tapped the microphone, which made an awful, loud sound. "Good morning!" she said. "May I have your attention, please? Let's get started with the announcements today!"

No one really ever listened to announcements. After morning meeting, your phone had to be in your locker for the whole day. If you were caught with it, you'd be in big, big trouble. Because we couldn't talk during morning meeting but it was our last chance to have our phones, we all just texted each other instead.

It was really quiet, and it wasn't long before I got a text from Lindsay, who was sitting with her BFF, Casey.

> Hey just checking in to see how ur family tree assignment is going?

I texted back,

> Haven't started!

Lindsay's reply came back a few seconds later.

> I figured u'd have it done by now! LOL

I didn't know what to text back. If I just sat down and did it, I could probably have it done pretty fast. I mean, it's not like I didn't know who was in my family. There were a couple third cousins whose names I'd need to double-check, maybe, but overall, I could spit out everyone who was at our last Fourth of July family barbecue . . . and there were more than fifty people there.

A minute went by. Then Lindsay texted again.

> R u upset by what Eric said? Bc he's just a moron.

Sometimes I can be more honest when I'm texting than when I talk.

> Yeah, a little. But I don't know why.

Lindsay's response came instantly.

> Do u want to talk about it?

I could see her looking at me, so I shook my head before texting back,

No. Not yet. But thanks.

Lindsey's response made me feel a little better.

Luv u, cousin. And I AM ur real cousin.

I smiled.

You are? Who is this?

Hahahahaha

After that the day went pretty fast. Last year we stayed in one classroom for most of the day, but in middle school we move classrooms for each period, so I kind of feel like once I settle into a class, it's time to get up and move again. It does make the day zoom by.

Kelsey and I usually walk home from school together, unless it's raining or really cold, and then Dad comes and picks us up. We usually walk with

Sophia and her sister and sometimes Casey and Riley, too, since we all live right near each other.

When my last class was over, I went to meet Kelsey, who was waiting for me in front of school, texting away.

"Ready?" she asked, without even looking up.

"Yeah," I said. "Let's go."

It's less than a ten-minute walk for us, and on a really crisp day like today, I was very happy to have some fresh air. Being outside always made me feel better. Even though it's such a short walk, Mom usually drives us because it's just easier for her to take us in the mornings.

"I totally got in trouble in Spanish class today," Kelsey said, blowing her bangs off her forehead.

"Why?" I asked.

"Because I didn't do my homework, and when Señora Diaz called on me, I had no idea what she was saying. She kept telling me I was messing up the pronouns and calling her a him."

I giggled.

"It wasn't funny," Kelsey said. Then she giggled too. "Señor, Señora, I mean, come on. There are more important things in life to worry about!"

"Well, if you can't speak the language properly, that is sort of an issue, Kels," I said. "The whole point of Spanish class is to learn to speak Spanish."

"If you were taking Spanish, it would be so much easier."

"I'm not doing your homework for you," I said.

"I'm not asking you to do my homework. I'd be asking you to help with my homework. There's a difference. In this family we help each other out. Mom always says that!" Kelsey protested.

I sighed and said nothing because I didn't want to start arguing with her, especially since we had just gotten home. I opened the screen door and stepped inside.

"Hi, Dad!" called Kelsey.

"Hello, my girls!" said Dad. "Good days?"

"It was okay," said Kelsey, eyeing me. "Mostly good."

"Mine too," I said.

"Hey, I heard you had a bad day yesterday," said Kelsey.

"Who did you hear that from?" I asked.

"Lindsay," said Kelsey. "She said Eric Sellers was a real jerk to you in history class."

"What happened?" asked Dad, looking worried.

"He's just a pest," I said. "It was just that he was annoying me. He also kept asking to go to the bathroom and kept interrupting Ms. Blueski. It was annoying all around."

Dad looked at me for a moment, then said, "Oh well, if that's all, that's not too bad. Unless he was annoying you specifically. Or on purpose."

I shrugged.

Kelsey was looking at me in a way that I could tell Lindsay had told her what happened. But unless she wanted me to spill on her episode in Spanish class, I knew she'd keep it to herself for now.

"Can we have a snack?" I asked.

"Right here," said Dad.

He had sliced some bananas in half the long way, and spread peanut butter on top. He had a cup of raisins we could sprinkle over them, which we used to call "ants on a log" because the raisins looked like ants on the banana log. But the idea of ants freaked Kelsey out, so he always put them on the side.

I flung some ants/raisins on top of the banana as Dad put down a plate of graham crackers.

"Yum," I said, making a sandwich.

"Today's practices start early," said Dad. "So I'm afraid you'll have to have your snack, then turn it right around."

"I hate rushing!" Kelsey whined.

"We're aware of that," said Dad. "Nobody likes to rush. That's why I'm telling you that there's still a half hour before we have to be anywhere. Jenna is already home, and she's taking you to field hockey practice."

Kelsey sighed and jumped off her chair, headed over to her knapsack, and took out a folder.

"What are you doing?" I asked.

"My Spanish homework," said Kelsey, giving me a scowl.

"Well, Kelsey, I am impressed," said Dad. "It will feel so good to get it out of the way early!"

If he only knew.

Chapter Seven
Ruby and Rusty

We had only a few practices before the first game, and I think everyone was a little anxious about it. Coach Wendy kept telling us that it didn't matter if we won, but the thing is, it feels much better to win than to lose. There's no denying that.

Coach Wendy likes us to stretch before we do drills, so I put my leg on the bench and leaned over to touch my toes.

"Hiya," Madeline said, her head upside down next to me. She was doing toe touches too, and was literally bent in half.

"Well, fancy seeing you down here!" I said, laughing. We both stood up.

"Ugh, I feel like my muscles are all tight," she said.

"Probably from sitting in class all day!"

Just then we heard barking, so we looked over. Mrs. Rose was walking three dogs around the track, and she waved.

"Ooh, puppies!" cried Isabella, and she went running over.

Madeline and I jogged behind her. By the time we caught up, Isabella was on her knees shrieking, and one of the cutest dogs I have ever seen was licking her face.

"Ruby, Ruby!" said Mrs. Rose, stroking the dog on the head. "She gets a little excited when she meets new people."

"Hi, Mrs. Rose!" I said. "Oh my goodness, that's her!"

It was the dog Mrs. Rose had shown me on her phone!

I dropped to my knees, and Ruby jumped over her leash to come lick my face too.

"I saw a picture of you," I said. "And I haven't stopped thinking about you!"

Ruby rolled over on her back.

"Do you want your tummy rubbed?" I asked her.

"She loves that," said Mrs. Rose, smiling. "And

yes, this is the adorable puppy you saw on my phone. She has a lot of energy. Don't you, Ruby?"

"Who is this?" asked Isabella, petting a dog that had climbed onto her lap.

"That's my Lucky," said Mrs. Rose. "And this . . . c'mon, sweetie. This one is shy." The third dog was behind Mrs. Rose. He almost looked like he was hiding. "This is Rusty."

"Rusty?" asked Madeline.

"Yes," said Mrs. Rose. "Most of the time we don't know the names of the dogs when they come to us, so we have to name them. This little guy was rescued from under some rocks, where a hiker found him, and we all admired his reddish brown fur, so we named him Rusty."

"Does he belong to anyone?" asked Isabella.

"Well, he probably did," said Mrs. Rose. "He's old enough that he wouldn't have been on his own this whole time."

"So someone just dropped him off somewhere?" I asked.

"Unfortunately, it does seem like that's what happened," said Mrs. Rose. "Sometimes people get overwhelmed if an animal doesn't fit into their family or they can't properly train it not to go to the bathroom in the house. And feeding an animal and paying for checkups definitely adds up."

"Well, what if he's just lost?" I asked.

"We definitely always hope we find the animal's home," said Mrs. Rose. "We put up posters and send e-mails and alert all the shelters and veterinarians' offices in the area. When the animal is truly lost, we usually are able to get them home within one or two days. We sent out a lot of alerts for Rusty, but it's been weeks and no one has claimed him."

"Poor Rusty!" said Madeline.

We were fussing over the dogs so much that we didn't hear Coach Wendy blowing her whistle.

"Girls!" she said, exasperated. "Practice is starting!"

We all said goodbye to the dogs, and I gave Ruby a kiss on the head. "You," I whispered. "I'm going to make you mine!"

I was paying attention during practice, but out of the corner of my eye I was also watching Mrs. Rose walk around the track. The three dogs listened to her and were all walking at about the same pace. Ruby was running ahead.

I didn't know how old Mrs. Rose was exactly,

but she could really power walk. And she must have walked a few miles during our practice.

After practice we were all panting, including the dogs. Ruby was tugging at her leash a little bit.

"Oh my," said Mrs. Rose. "This dog could walk all day and not tire out!"

"Can I take her around once?" I asked eagerly.

I saw Dad and Kelsey approaching the soccer field from the parking lot, but I figured I could get one quick lap in before we had to head home.

"You know, if you could run her once, that'd be great," said Mrs. Rose. "I don't really run, and this puppy seems to need a little bit more that I can do."

"No problem!" I grinned. I had never walked a dog before, so I took the leash but wasn't sure if I should pull it or not. I looked at Mrs. Rose.

"You don't want to pull or tug too hard," said Mrs. Rose. "Think of the leash more as a guide, so you show her what direction you want her to go."

I nodded and started to run. In half a second Ruby was at my ankles, running with me. But soon the leash was getting tangled around my legs, and she kept running in front of me, then behind me.

She was yapping so much that I almost didn't hear

Mrs. Rose calling, "Rusty! Rusty!" behind me.

I turned my head and Rusty, the shy dog, was bolting toward me, his leash trailing behind him. Mrs. Rose was half running, half power walking to try to catch up to him.

Just then Dad sprinted down to the track. Rusty saw him following and really took off. That dog was fast. But so was Dad. Dad and Rusty were running together around the track, and if you didn't know that Dad was trying to catch him, it looked like they were actually playing a game. Rusty kept looking at Dad, then pulling ahead a little bit. Dad would catch up and Rusty would take off again, like a big game of chase. But Rusty didn't take off so far ahead of Dad. He seemed to want to stay with him.

Finally, Dad and Rusty went all the way around the track. Rusty saw Mrs. Rose waiting for him and slowed down, and Dad was able to grab his leash. Ruby and I finished our lap, Ruby yapping all the way. Kelsey was standing next to Mrs. Rose.

"Oh my goodness," said Mrs. Rose, panting. "Well, that was a workout I didn't expect!"

"This dog can run," said Dad admiringly, petting Rusty's head.

"Who knew?" said Mrs. Rose. "He's been so quiet and timid. That's the first time I think we've seen a little bit of his personality come out."

Rusty looked up at Dad and closed his eyes. "Runners can always find each other," said Dad, scratching Rusty under the chin.

"Ohhhhh," said Kelsey, patting Ruby. "Dad, Molly was right. This dog is the cutest!"

"She's pretty cute," said Dad, still petting Rusty.

"Molly has always wanted a dog," said Kelsey. "So, you know, this one . . ."

"First of all, we've talked about this," said Dad. "A dog is a huge responsibility and a lot of work."

"It is a big responsibility," said Mrs. Rose. "And it's important to think through. Not thinking it through leads to situations like poor Rusty."

Rusty didn't look sad exactly, but he did sort of look like he was worried. "You have just the right touch with him, Chris," said Mrs. Rose.

"Molly and I both love dogs," said Dad.

"Well, now that I see how he can run, I wish I could run with him more regularly," said Mrs. Rose. "I may reach out and see if anyone in the rescue group runs, so I can pair him up with someone."

Family Recipe

Dad looked like he was mulling something over.

"Well," he said, then stopped.

We all looked at him.

"Molly has been telling me to get my runs in while she has soccer practice. I think it's her way of trying to distract her embarrassing dad."

I rolled my eyes.

"But if I could bring Rusty to practices, then I can get my workout in, and we'd be able to get Rusty a run in too."

Rusty perked up his ears and stood up.

"Ah, you like to run!" said Dad to Rusty in a mushy baby voice. Kelsey and I started laughing.

"Well, that would be super," said Mrs. Rose. "If you can manage it, I'd love to take you up on that offer!"

As Dad and Mrs. Rose looked at their schedules on their phones and coordinated Rusty's runs, Kelsey and I took turns petting Ruby.

"Isn't she the sweetest?" I said, sighing.

"She's super cute," said Kelsey.

"Wouldn't you love to come live with us?" I said to Ruby, pulling her onto my lap. She settled in, then jumped up again and went chasing after a squirrel.

Kelsey and I ran after her, and then I ran ahead, blocking her, and Kelsey scooped her up. "You are a handful!" she said breathlessly.

"She's totally going to be ours," I said to Kelsey.

Kelsey said, "Mom will never say yes."

"We'll see," I said, already dreaming of Ruby snuggling next to me in bed at night.

Chapter Eight
Family Love

We got home a few minutes later than planned, and Jenna and Mom were already getting dinner on the table.

"I got dinner started!" said Mom, and the four of us looked at each other. "It seemed like a good fall night to start with soup, so I brought some of Nans's squash soup home from the restaurant."

We all looked relieved.

"And I stopped and picked up a loaf of bread and a salad," Mom said.

"That sounds like a perfect fall dinner," said Dad.

"And Nans sent home more apple pie for taste testing. Since Molly told her it was perfect, she's obsessed with making it absolutely perfect," Mom said. "She made about five pies today and told me to bring this one home to see if 'perfect can get more perfect.' Oh, and she said to put ice cream on top of it. Vanilla, if possible."

"Well if she said to add ice cream, I guess we'll have to add ice cream," said Kelsey.

We sat down and Mom said, "Let's do best and worst."

Best and worst is a thing Mom and Dad do at dinner: each person has to tell the best and worst thing that happened that day. We do the worst part because as Mom always says, sometimes bad comes with the good, but that's okay.

"I'll go first," said Jenna. "Best is that I'll be doing a piano solo in the fall recital. Worst is that now I have tennis, tutoring, work, and a solo to study for."

"Jenna, that's wonderful!" said Mom. "A solo is a big mark of excellence and confidence from your teacher."

"Well, my best thing today was playing with an adorable dog that Molly says we're going to adopt," said Kelsey.

"What?" said Mom, looking at Dad.

"Oh, no, no, no," said Dad. "I said it was not a

good time for us to adopt a pet. And I meant it."

"Well, then I guess the worst part is that we aren't getting a dog," said Kelsey, looking at me.

"It's not fair!" I said. Suddenly I was just really frustrated. "I can take care of a dog. I'll need help buying food and taking her to the vet, but otherwise I don't need anyone's help!"

"Sweetie," said Dad. "I love you, but I saw you today and you could barely walk that dog yourself, let alone take care of it yourself."

"Where were you walking a dog?" asked Jenna.

"Mrs. Rose was walking her three dogs around the track while she had soccer practice," Dad said.

"What's your best thing?" Mom asked me.

I sulked a little and didn't answer. I knew getting a dog was a lot of work, and I knew Mom had already said no, but I'd had a bad week, and it was getting worse. "Nothing," I said. "Nothing was good today."

"Find one good thing," said Dad.

I dug in. I knew I was kind of acting like a baby, but tonight I was just not in the mood to play this game. "Nope."

"So your day was so terrible that not even one little good thing happened?" said Dad.

They all looked at me.

"Are you upset because of the Eric thing?" asked Kelsey.

I glared at her.

"Okay, now this is the second time I've heard 'the Eric thing' come up today. What is going on?" Dad said. He and Mom were looking at me.

"You brought it up, Kelsey," I said. "So you tell them."

I was mad at Kelsey, but honestly, I was a teeny-tiny bit grateful. I didn't know how to tell them about what was going on with the family tree. So I let Kelsey do it.

Kelsey sighed. "Lindsay told me. She was worried about Molly."

"What is it?" asked Mom, her voice getting a little high.

"In history class we have to do a project with a family tree," said Kelsey. "It's supposed to be a lesson where we learn more about our family history and how it shaped us. Ms. Blueski said history can be about wars and stuff, but it can also be personal."

"And?" said Dad.

"Eric Sellers told Molly that her tree wasn't real.

He said that because she was adopted, she had a real family and us, who I guess aren't her real family. Molly got upset and ran out of class," Kelsey finished.

It is not usually quiet in our house. Jenna is loud, Kelsey is always talking or singing, and Dad often hums or has music playing. Mom is always moving around doing something.

But just then it was silent, and we all sat there staring at our food. I could hear the *tick tick tick* of the grandfather clock in the front hall.

Then Dad said, "Oh, Molly!" and burst into tears.

"This is not about you, Mr. Goo," said Mom.

"It's about my daughter!" said Dad, sniffing into his napkin.

"Okay," said Mom. "Kelsey heard this from Lindsay. I don't like playing the telephone game with things like this. Molly, can you please tell us exactly what happened?"

I didn't want to talk about it, but I knew if I didn't, they'd never let it go. And also I had no idea how to handle Eric. Or the feeling I had in my stomach, all tight and queasy.

"Eric Sellers asked me if I was adding my 'real mom' to my family tree, because Mom wasn't my real mom. Lindsay turned around and told him that Mom was real and not fake, but he kind of wouldn't let it go. I didn't run out of class. I just left quickly when it was over."

"All right," said Dad, blowing his nose. "Let's break this down. First of all, you are our real daughter, and Mom and I are your real parents."

"I know that," I said.

"Good," said Dad. "You are adopted, but you know that, too."

"I do recall being told that, yes," I said.

Dad stifled a laugh. "You do have biological parents, and a mother who gave birth to you."

"I know that, too," I said.

"Okay," said Dad. "Now, sometimes people say stupid things, but not because they're trying to be awful. It's because they have questions, but they don't know how to sensitively ask them. Do you think that might be the case with Eric? That maybe he's just curious about your family tree?"

I thought about that a second.

"Maybe," said Kelsey. "He's not a bad person; he's just, like, the most annoying kid in the class."

"Molly?" asked Dad.

"I don't know," I said. "But he upset me."

"Are you upset because he was rude, or are you upset because you didn't know how to answer him?" asked Mom.

Bingo. The thing about Mom is that somehow she always knows what I'm feeling.

I looked at her. "Yes," I whispered. "Both."

"Okay. The simple answer is that, yes, you are adopted. And technically you have a biological mother, who gave birth to you, and me, the person you call Mom, who actually is your mother."

I nodded.

Mom continued. "What's important on this tree isn't just the facts of it, although there are, of course, facts. The tree is about your family. The family tree can represent your history in whatever way you feel is best."

"Isn't history based on facts?" Kelsey asked.

"Well, yes, but the fact is that Mom and I are Molly's parents," said Dad. "So if she lists that, then it's factually correct. If Molly also lists her biological mother, that's factually correct too. But she can also leave her out if she's not comfortable discussing that."

"But how factual is it if she leaves out some facts?"

asked Jenna. "I mean, she should put everything she knows in the tree."

I felt like everyone was talking about me, but nobody was talking to me. Suddenly I felt the same way I had in class, like I just had to get out of there. I pushed my chair away and ran out the front door.

Chapter Nine
Nature Vs. Nurture

I sat down on the front step, not sure what to do next. A few minutes later the door opened. Dad threw my sneakers on the step.

"C'mon," he said. He was already wearing his running shoes and was carrying more gear.

I put my sneakers on. "Where are we going?" I asked.

Dad jogged down the front walk. He put on his reflective jacket and headlamp and handed me one of each too. I guess they were Mom's.

"Sometimes when you feel like running, the best thing to do is actually run," said Dad. "Let's go."

I followed him down the path, out into the quiet street, and the two of us took off. We just ran, side by side, a nice slow pace, not saying anything for a long while.

"Look at those stars," said Dad.

I looked up and he was right. There were a ton of stars. It was crisp and cool, and it felt good breathing in the night air.

We jogged around the neighborhood. I followed Dad as we ran past Casey's house. I could see her sitting at her desk in her bedroom. I wondered if she was texting Lindsay. The two of them were best friends.

There's one road in our neighborhood that leads to a dead end. If you go on the trail, it leads to the lake. We reached the dead end and Dad turned around. Someone had their windows open, and you could hear music and people's voices.

I heard a kid shout, "Nooooo," and I wondered if it was one of the Sherer kids since they lived in our neighborhood.

I was waiting for Dad to try to talk about things. I kept looking at him, but he was just looking straight ahead. Maybe he was waiting for me to start talking. But there was something really nice about being together in silence. We were both breathing hard, and all I could hear was the *slap slap* of our sneakers hitting the pavement. I felt my body begin to relax.

When we finally came back up our street, I was tired. We reached our driveway, and Dad turned off his headlamp.

He smiled. "You have the running bug!" he said. "I'm sorry to say there's no cure. But running regularly definitely helps."

I laughed. "It must be genetic!" Then I stopped. "Dad, how can I tell what's genetic and what I just pick up from you and Mom?"

Dad went up the front walk, and I followed him.

"Well," he said, sitting down on the step. "There's something called nature versus nurture. Nature means what you are genetically predetermined to do or have, like brown eyes or a tall frame. Nurture is more about what affects you growing up, like what language is spoken at home, if you live in a city or a small town, or what your family does on the weekends. If, say, you grow up in a family who cooks a lot, you might be more likely to cook."

"Well, nature or nurture, I'm not getting any cooking skills from Mom," I said, sitting down next to him.

"No," said Dad. "But you might get her love of eating together as a family, or the importance she puts on fresh foods."

I nodded. "Which matters more?"

"There's a lot of debate about that," said Dad. "There's no definitive answer, but they both affect you."

"So maybe my biological father was a runner?"

"Possibly," said Dad. "Or your biological mother. But Mom and I are also runners, so it's unclear whether that's nature or nurture."

I sighed.

"I'm sorry this week was hard for you," said Dad. "Mom and I are always worried that you might have questions, but we don't always think about the questions other people might have about you."

"Yeah," I said. I tightened my fists, just like my stomach was tightening.

"What is it?" Dad asked.

"It's just weird to think there's this other family out there. I never really thought about it like that. Like, is there a person walking around wondering about me?"

"Maybe," Dad said. "In terms of your adoption, we

don't have a lot of details. We know your biological mother's name but not your biological father's name. And your bio mom's name is a very common name in South Korea. We tried to find out more information so we'd have it for you, but we've come up short. We have her medical history that she gave the adoption agency, but that doesn't say anything about, like, what her favorite food was, or if she liked to play soccer."

We'd gone through my story many times before. My biological mother put me up for adoption when I was a few weeks old. We don't know exactly why, but she was very young, and Mom and Dad thought maybe she wasn't ready or prepared to become a mother.

I was also born with an eye condition that required me to have surgery when I was about a year old. It went fine, but I still wear glasses now to see a movie or to see the whiteboard in class. It wasn't major surgery, but hearing that a baby needs surgery can be scary. Maybe that had something to do with my birth mother's decision too.

I lived in a house run by an adoption agency for a few months until Mom and Dad flew to South Korea to bring me home. We have the picture on the mantel of Jenna holding me at the airport, wearing a BIG SISTER T-shirt. Nans and Grandpa were there, and Grandma, my dad's mother, and PopPop, my dad's father, too.

Everyone looked happy except for me. I was really red in the face and crying.

Mom opened the door and peeked out. "Oh, you're back!" she said. She came out and sat on the step next to me. "I do not like you running at night," she said.

"Who, me?" said Dad.

"Well, you, too, but mainly Molly. Cars speed on these streets."

"We stayed in the neighborhood," I said. "And we wore our headlamps so people could see us."

"I'm your mom," Mom said. "I worry."

"Do you think my biological mother worries?" I asked.

Mom thought for a second. "I don't know if 'worry' is the right word," she said. "But she probably thinks about you. I hope she knows that you are safe and loved and that you're mostly happy. Or at least that's what we tell her when we write her."

Every year Mom and Dad wrote a letter to my

biological mother with details about what I was learning or doing or interested in and a picture of me. They sent it to the adoption agency, who had them translated into Korean and said they would keep the letters in case my bio mom reached out and wanted to know more about me.

"Maybe I can help write the one this year," I said.

"That'd be great," Mom said. "In your own voice."

"Always in your own voice," said Dad. "That's the best way to be."

"So my voice and version over facts?"

"No," said Dad, knowing I was thinking about the family tree project. "Facts are facts. You have a biological mother and father, and that's part of your history. But how you define your family is really up to you. We have friends you call aunt and uncle, for instance, who aren't your 'real' aunt and uncle."

That was true. Aunt Miranda and Uncle Albert were Mom and Dad's best friends from college. We weren't related to them, but they acted like our aunt and uncle. They were at holidays and birthday parties, they had pictures of us on their refrigerator. And sometimes when Mom and Dad had to work, Aunt Miranda stayed with me if I was sick. This whole family thing was getting more complicated.

"You have a family that you are born into and you have a family that you create throughout your life," said Mom. "When I married Dad, I got this whole other part of a family that I hadn't even known before."

I nodded. "So your family keeps growing?"

"Yes," said Dad. "Your mom and dad stay the same, and your siblings, but outside that, your family really expands."

"But no matter what," said Mom, "you will always have Dad and me, and Kelsey and Jenna."

"Speaking of which," Dad said, motioning behind him. Kelsey and Jenna were looking out the window at us.

"I'm guessing Kelsey is worried that you're telling me she got in trouble in her Spanish class today," said Mom, smirking.

"She told you?" I said.

"She felt bad that she told us about Eric, so she spilled when you and Dad went out for a run."

"What?" said Dad.

"Kelsey didn't do her Spanish homework and got in trouble in class," I said. "She also mixed up the pronouns and called Señora Diaz a man."

Dad laughed. He motioned to Kelsey and Jenna, who came out and sat on the bottom step, right in front of us.

"You know what the best part of my day was?" Dad asked.

"This!" said Mom.

"Yes!" said Dad. "Sitting here on a beautiful night under the stars with everyone I love most in the world."

"And you know the best thing about the best part coming later at night?" Mom asked.

"What?" asked Jenna.

"The worst parts of our days are behind us."

"Let's end it on a high note, gang," said Dad. "It's getting late, and we have school and work tomorrow. Tomorrow is another day."

Tomorrow was another day indeed.

Chapter Ten
Eric Is Still Annoying!

I felt better the next morning after talking to Mom and Dad the night before, but I was still dreading going to history class. I took a deep breath as I entered the classroom.

"Okay, everyone," said Ms. Blueski. "Let's take out the trees. You should all have the basic information filled in. At this stage you should be talking to your family members to find out stories that you may not know."

Everyone took out their trees. I laid mine on my desk and stared at it. So far I had only Kelsey and Jenna on it.

Eric leaned over. "So how many moms and dads did you put on there?" he asked.

Lindsay whipped around. "Eric, mind your own business!" she said.

"Hey, I asked Molly, not you!" said Eric.

"Mind your own business, Eric," I said.

He looked surprised. "But I just wanted to know where you were putting your real mom!"

"My real mom is right here," I said, writing Mom's name. "And here is my real dad." I wrote his name too.

"But what about your other mother?" said Eric.

"I don't have another mother, Eric!" I yelled.

"What's going on over there?" called Ms. Blueski.

"Molly is very sensitive," said Eric in a high voice.

The whole class turned around. I could feel my eyes get really teary, but I didn't want to cry. I swallowed hard.

Ms. Blueski came and stood in front of my desk. "You okay, Molly?" she asked softly.

I nodded.

"Ms. Blueski, Eric is pestering Molly about her tree," said Lindsay.

"Because she's adopted, so her tree is complicated!" said Eric.

Ms. Blueski closed her eyes for a second. "Okay,"

she said. "I hadn't thought about that coming up." She bit her lip and looked at me, then knelt down. "If you are uncomfortable with this project, we can think of another one for you to do."

I was aware that everyone was looking at me. I shook my head. "I'm fine with it. I know who my family is."

Ms. Blueski nodded. "Good. But you let me know if I can help." Then she turned around. "You, Eric, need to make sure you get your tree done before you start worrying about everyone else's. Please leave Molly to her own tree."

Ms. Blueski walked back up to the front of the class again, and everyone went back to their project. I just sat there.

Lindsay turned around. "Everything all right?" she asked.

I wanted to crawl under my desk, and I must have looked like it.

"Molly, it's okay," Lindsay said firmly. "It's going to be okay."

I hoped she was right.

☀ ☀ ☀ ☀ ☀

After school we had our last soccer practice before the game, and everyone was a little nervous.

Dad had been meeting Mrs. Rose, as they'd discussed. After dropping me off at practice, he'd take Rusty to do laps. Rusty seemed to be listening when Dad slowed down or told him to stop. Dad seemed to be having a lot of fun.

Coach Wendy was making us do running drills. You had to run down the field, stop, then come back through a lane of orange cones. It seemed easy, but running around the cones meant you had to pull your body in tight or you'd trip.

"That's it, that's it!" said Coach. "Be aware, be aware!"

Riley was running behind me. I heard "ooof" and turned around to see her sprawled out on the grass.

I held out my hand and helped her up. "Um," I said. "You have some grass in your hair."

"Oh, boy," she said. "I don't know whether to laugh or cry."

I giggled. "Laugh?" I said.

She shook her head and the grass sprayed all around.

"It happens," I said.

"Well, I hope it doesn't happen at the game tomorrow," said Riley. "I just get so nervous! When I just play, I'm fine. When I think about it, I fall!"

"If you fall," I said, "you get back up. We've all fallen during a game."

"Thanks," said Riley. "Maybe Kelsey was right and I should have done field hockey instead."

"Kelsey told you what sport to do?" I said, surprised.

"No," said Riley. "We were all planning on trying out for field hockey, but then I decided to do soccer with Isabella instead, and I think she was disappointed."

This is when it gets weird to have your sister in your grade. I knew Kelsey wasn't just disappointed; she was really angry at Riley, and I knew she was hurt that Riley had decided to play soccer. She had been moping and stomping around the house for a week about how middle school changed everything.

"Well," I said, "the thing is that Kelsey gets over things quickly."

This was true, so it was easy to smile reassuringly at Riley.

"She'll be at the game on Saturday cheering you

on. Friends root for each other," I added.

"I know," said Riley. "She's a good friend." Then she turned to me. "You know, everyone says you say the craziest things sometimes, but I think you always say exactly the right thing."

I smiled again, and we jogged back for the team huddle.

Coach Wendy went over a few things, like playing our zone and being aware on the field. "It's not just you running down to make a goal," she said. "This is a team sport. So let's all be aware of our teammates and where they are, so we can pass properly, and line up our offense or defense."

As we were packing up our bags, I saw Dad talking to Mrs. Rose, who held Lucky's leash. Dad had Rusty on a leash, and Ruby was running around him in circles.

I shoved my cleats in my bag, because Mom freaks out if I wear them in the house and track in clumps of grass. I quickly tore off my socks, slipped my flip-flops on and ran to Ruby.

"Ruby!" I called, and she came bounding over.

"Ruby is ready," said Mrs. Rose, and I noticed she was carrying a large tote bag.

Mrs. Rose looked at Dad.

He grinned. "Ruby is coming for a sleepover!"

"Ruby is coming to live with us!" I shrieked.

"No, no, no!" said Dad. "She's coming for a sleepover while Mrs. Rose does an overnight shift at the hospital."

"I have to do a few overnight shifts each month," said Mrs. Rose. "Usually another person in my group takes the dogs, but your dad volunteered!"

"So both dogs?" I said, eyeing Rusty, who was patiently sitting at Dad's feet.

"Yep," said Dad. "Lucky stays with his dog walker."

"That's what the old dog is used to," said Mrs. Rose, rubbing his head.

"This way we can have some company over the weekend, and you can see exactly what having a dog entails," said Dad.

"So if it goes well, we get to keep Ruby?" I said excitedly.

"No," said Dad. "We've been pretty clear on that, Molly."

We'll see, I thought. *If this goes really well, then maybe they'll see that we are a dog family after all.*

Chapter Eleven
From No Dogs to Two!

"Let's load them up!" said Dad.

I took Ruby's leash and she ran off, streaking ahead of me. I had to pull on her leash, and I guess I pulled a little hard, because she yelped.

"Oh, I'm sorry!" I said.

"Here," said Dad, giving me Rusty's leash. He bent down and scooped up Ruby, who started licking his face. "This one is literally a handful!"

We got into the car and Rusty sat in the back seat, looking out the window. Ruby was running from the front seat to the back seat, barking.

Mrs. Rose was waving good-bye as she got into her car with Lucky.

"Ruby's excited!" I said.

"She's nuts," sighed Dad.

Ruby jumped behind the back seat and wedged herself up against the back window.

"Can you see?" I asked Dad.

"Yeah," said Dad. "I just hope I don't have to stop short."

"Does Mom know this is happening?" I asked, a little nervously.

"Of course!" said Dad. "We discuss everything."

When we got home, I took Ruby off her leash and she bolted through the back door and into the kitchen.

I heard Kelsey scream, and then I heard a crash.

"This dog just ran under my feet and tripped me!" yelled Kelsey.

The plate was broken and there were cheese cubes all over the floor.

"Okay, let me help," I said. I wanted everything to go just right for this visit.

I got the dustpan out of the closet and swept up the pieces of the plate and the cheese, except a cube that Ruby was batting around like a ball.

"You'd better get that," said Jenna. "She can choke on that if she tries to eat it."

Choke? Oh no.

I hurriedly reached down, but Ruby thought we were playing a game and snapped up the cheese.

"Drop that, Ruby!" I said.

I swear she smiled at me as she ran into the family room. I chased her from the family room to the living room to the dining room, where I cornered her, picked her up, and grabbed the cheese out of her mouth.

She was either a little miffed about that or she thought we were playing, because then she nipped my fingers.

"Ouch!" I squealed.

It didn't hurt, but I was surprised. Unfortunately, because I was surprised, I also dropped Ruby, who whimpered.

"Oh, Ruby!" I said, feeling immediately awful. "Are you okay?"

Jenna came in and looked at her. "Can you walk to me, Ruby?" she asked.

Ruby whimpered more, and I started to panic, my heart beating fast.

"Come here, pretty baby," said Jenna in a soothing voice.

Ruby got up and skittered over to her.

"Okay, she's walking. I think you just startled her," Jenna said.

"Well she startled me by biting me!" I said.

"She bit you?" said Dad, who must have come in during the commotion.

"She just nipped," I said quickly, immediately feeling a little defensive. "I think she thought we were playing. She didn't do it on purpose."

"This one is a wild one," said Jenna.

"You seem to have a way with her," said Dad.

As Jenna held Ruby, she calmed down.

"This is a new place for both dogs, so they're probably a little nervous. Let's try to make them comfortable," Dad said.

"Where's Rusty?" I asked.

"By the door," Dad said. "I could barely nudge him out of the car, and now he won't come into the house."

Rusty was standing right in the doorway. I never knew a dog could look worried, but boy, he did.

I bent down and whispered into his ear, "It's okay, Rusty. This is your home for this weekend, and we'll take care of you!"

He looked at me, and I think he was a little reassured, because he sat down.

"Okay," said Dad, running his hands through his hair. "This is going to be hard work and require some team effort. Let's get the dogs fed, since it's almost dinnertime."

Dad peered into the bag Mrs. Rose had given him and took out four stacked dog bowls. He opened two cans of dog food and spooned them into two bowls.

"Ah, Mrs. Rose thought of everything," he said, and he pulled out what looked like a place mat and put it on the floor. "Okay, Kels, fill the other bowls with some cold water and put them on the mat too."

Ruby and Rusty watched us. When Dad put the dog bowls down with the food, Ruby started wiggling and yelping in Jenna's arms.

"Are you hungry, baby?" Jenna asked, and placed Ruby in front of her dinner.

Ruby ran around the mat a few times, then hungrily started eating.

Rusty seemed a little wary. He didn't move and instead watched Ruby gulp down her food.

"C'mon, Rusty," I said, holding up the bowl. "This one's for you."

Rusty looked at me and then the bowl. Slowly he walked over to the bowl, lowered his head, and took a little bite. Then he looked up. We were all looking at him.

"You have an audience, Rusty," said Dad, laughing.

I guess Rusty realized he was hungry too, because then he started eating faster and faster, licking the bowl when the food was gone.

"Okay, now the humans," said Dad. He opened the refrigerator and took out a bunch of stuff to make a salad. "Jenna, can you boil a pot of water for pasta?"

Jenna filled the pasta pot and Dad started sautéing tomatoes for the sauce.

As soon as Ruby finished, she kicked her bowl over, and the gravy from her food splattered everywhere.

"Eeeuuuww!" yelled Kelsey. "Dog food is on the wall!"

"Well, you'll have to clean that up," said Dad, chopping away.

I got a wet towel and wiped down the wall and the floor.

Ruby was running around the kitchen table.

"In a way I guess it's good that Mom isn't home yet to see this mess," I said, looking around.

"You want to race?" teased Kelsey, who playfully started chasing Ruby.

I guess Ruby got a little wound up, because the next thing we knew, she peed all over the floor.

"Gross!" Kelsey screamed, jumping up on a chair. "It's all over the floor!"

Dad sighed and put down the knife. "Okay, girls, we need a bucket and some paper towels. I'll get the cleaner."

Kelsey didn't move. I went to the closet and pulled out the mop and bucket. Dad squirted the floor with the cleaning fluid, and I squatted down to help wipe it up. It was pretty easy.

Ruby was yelping and trying to jump up to the chair Kelsey was still standing on.

"Ruby, Ruby," said Dad. "Shhhhh . . . and Kelsey, come down from there!"

Kelsey came down and Ruby stopped yelping.

Rusty had finished his dinner and was sitting next to his bowl.

"What now?" I said to Dad.

"What?" he said, a little flustered. "Why don't you and Kelsey take the dogs out to the yard and play while Jenna helps me with dinner?"

"C'mon, boy," I said to Rusty, who slowly followed me outside.

Kelsey was right behind me, with Ruby racing to beat us. We went down the back steps into the yard.

Other than having catches with Mom and Dad, I hadn't really played in the backyard in a long time. We still had a tire swing and a fort that Dad had built us, but neither seemed quite right for dogs.

Kelsey picked up a tennis ball that was lying in the grass. "Hey, maybe they'll like this," she said.

She tossed the ball to Ruby, who tried to pick it up in her mouth. It was too big for her, so she was kind of wrestling with it, and she totally fell over it.

"Grrrrrr," she growled.

"Hey, Rusty, do you want to play?" I asked.

Rusty was watching Ruby curiously. I ran to the shed and got the bucket of tennis balls we had in there from Jenna's tennis lessons.

"Here, Rusty!" I said, tossing a ball to him.

He was about to go chase it, but Ruby beat him to it, growling and batting the ball around with her paws.

"Hey, that was for Rusty!" Kelsey said. "You are a piggy puppy!"

Family Recipe

Every ball I threw to Rusty, Ruby went after, leaving a bunch of balls lying in the grass around us.

Finally, I picked one up and went over to Rusty. "Here, boy," I said. "This one is for you."

He nudged it out of my hand. I threw it up in the air and he jumped for it, going up on his hind legs. I caught it, then tossed it a little farther. He ran for it and caught it in his mouth.

"Good catch, Rusty!" I said.

I guess that made Ruby a little jealous, because she came bounding over, nipping at Rusty.

"Kelsey, throw her a ball of her own!" I said.

"Look at this!" I heard Mom say over the fence.

I guess we hadn't heard her pull up in the driveway, but she opened the gate and Ruby went running over to her.

As Mom leaned down, Ruby licked her face.

"Oh, so you know exactly who to butter up!" said Mom, laughing.

Rusty sat next to me, watching.

"Is this Rusty?" asked Mom. She patted him on the head. "I hear you're going to run with us tomorrow!"

Rusty barked, which must have been his version of "yes."

We made our way back into the house for dinner. With all the excitement, I hadn't realized it was a little later than usual, and I was hungry.

As soon as we sat down, Ruby began to yelp, putting her paws on my lap.

"What do you want?" I asked.

"She wants your dinner," said Dad. "Some dogs are fed scraps from the table, which is not something we're going to do. Plus, Mrs. Rose said she was trying to cure Ruby of this habit."

"Want to do best and worst?" Mom said.

But every time we started to talk, Ruby would yelp and run around. It was kind of a chaotic dinner after a long day.

I cleared my place and was looking forward to going upstairs and chilling out when Dad said, "Okay, let's go."

"Go where?" I asked.

"Dogs need to be walked a lot," Dad said. "And …," he said, handing Kelsey and me each a plastic bag. "Dogs mean you have to go on poop patrol!"

"What are these for?" asked Kelsey.

Dad grinned. "When the dogs poop, we have to clean up after them."

Kelsey shrieked. "You mean we have to pick it up? That is so, so gross!"

"It's not gross," said Dad. "It's part of having a dog. You have to take care of them and clean up after them!"

We got the dogs on their leashes and started off down the street. Of course Ruby pooped in about five minutes.

Dad looked at me. "Well, you wanted a dog. . . ."

I sighed and got out the baggie. Dad showed me how to turn it inside out to hold the poop through the bag so I wouldn't have to touch it. I kind of held my nose and did it quick. I dropped the baggie into the bigger bag Dad had brought. It wasn't great, but it wasn't terrible.

I can do this, I thought.

Three poops later I was beginning to wonder if having a dog was worth it. Ruby kept pulling at my leash, and I was starting to get chilly.

"C'mon," I said. "Let's go home."

"Rusty hasn't gone yet," said Dad. "One more block."

I sighed.

"Hey, at least it's autumn," said Dad. "Just think

about doing this three times a day in the middle of winter when it's sleeting outside."

Kelsey put her arm around me and squeezed. Dad walked on the other side and put his arm around me too. Rusty finally pooped and the three of us walked the dogs home.

"Molly," Kelsey said as we turned onto our street. "I love you and I'm glad you're my sister. And if we ever get a dog, I won't fight you on it. I won't ask you to share it."

"Okay . . . ," I said.

"Because," she said, "cleaning up poop has to be one of the grossest things ever, and I promise you I'm never doing it. That dog will be all yours."

"Thanks, sis," I said, squeezing her back. "Or should I say *gracias*?"

"Ugh," Kelsey said, giving me an annoyed look. "Let's pick up the pace. I still have Spanish homework to do."

Chapter Twelve

Teamwork—at Home
and on the Field

We all woke up really tired, and that's because Ruby kept the whole house up most of the night.

Dad had thought it would be best for Ruby and Rusty to sleep in the laundry room, even though I tried to convince him that Ruby should sleep with me. Rusty lay down and went to sleep quickly. But Ruby yelped, whined, and scratched the door.

Finally, Dad went down and tried to pet her and soothe her to get her to sleep in her dog bed that Mrs. Rose had sent. But Ruby would not sleep.

After midnight, Mom went downstairs and brought Ruby up to my room. She put Ruby on the bed, where she happily curled up.

"Good night, girls," whispered Mom.

I put my head down on the pillow, happy with Ruby sleeping on my feet.

But an hour later Ruby was up again. She was chewing on an old stuffed animal in my room and was running around with it.

This went on until Dad came in and took Ruby downstairs again.

Jenna opened her door and yelled, "That dog is keeping me up!"

Mom and Dad took turns all night. Dad even texted Mrs. Rose, who told them that Ruby was frequently up a lot in the night

We were all bleary-eyed at breakfast.

"It's like having a baby that's been up all night," moaned Mom. She poured some more coffee.

Dad yawned. "Molly, are you ready for your soccer game today?"

I nodded. "All set except for my cleats," I said, standing up.

I had already put on my uniform, even my shin guards and socks. I wanted to be ready.

"Thatta girl," said Dad. "Bring on the soccer game!" Then he yawned again.

"Have another cup of coffee, Chris," said Mom.

Kelsey came stomping down the stairs. "I. Am. So. Tired! I don't care how cute that dog is," she said, glaring. "She kept me up all night!"

"It was not a great night," said Mom. "But you girls are seeing firsthand how much getting a dog affects the whole family in many different ways."

"Well, maybe we could just get a dog who sleeps," said Jenna, putting her head on her arms.

"When do they go back to Mrs. Rose?" asked Kelsey.

"Tomorrow afternoon," said Dad.

"We have another night with them?" Kelsey yelped. "Can I sleep over at Sophia's house?"

"Maybe it will be easier now that the dogs are more used to the house," said Mom.

We all looked at her doubtfully.

"We should get going soon," said Dad. "Molly, you have warm-up in half an hour."

I went into the laundry room to get my cleats. I rummaged around. Finally, I lifted up Ruby's dog bed and then let out a huge yell. "RUBY!"

Everyone came running.

I held up my cleats, which were both chewed all the way through. The laces were in tatters, and there were teeth marks and little holes all over them.

"Uh-oh," said Kelsey.

"Oh boy," said Mom.

I stormed out of the room into the family room, where Ruby was blissfully sleeping on Mom's favorite chair.

"Whatever you do," said Jenna, "I beg you not to wake her up."

"But it's the first game of the season!" I wailed. "These were broken in just right! And the rules say I need to wear cleats for the game. What am I going to do?"

Kelsey's feet were a least a size smaller than mine, so I couldn't wear hers.

Mom grabbed her phone. "I'm texting around to see if anyone has a spare pair," she said. "The sporting goods store doesn't open until ten, and the game starts at nine thirty."

"Agggghhhh," I said, sitting down on the floor. "Why is everything so hard right now?" I felt like I was going to cry.

A few minutes later, Elizabeth Ellis's mom texted back that she had an extra pair in my size. They were brand-new and all mine.

"Brand-new!" Dad said. "That's lucky!"

I looked at him. "Like brand-new running shoes?"

Cleats, like running shoes, sometimes hurt when they were new and stiff. They felt a lot better once you'd worn them a few times and they kind of molded to your feet.

"Well, you'll have to break them in," said Dad, picking up my destroyed cleats. "It's better than wearing these. We can pick Elizabeth's up on the way to the game."

It took us forever to get into the car, because the whole family was coming for the first game and because Mom and Dad thought it was better to bring Rusty and Ruby with us. I think they were afraid of what Ruby would do to the house if we left her there alone.

Rusty got in the back with us, but Ruby decided to hop around the car. Finally, Dad kind of tackled her and got into the front passenger seat.

"GO!" he said to Mom, and we finally pulled out of the driveway.

We stopped to pick up the new cleats, and by the time we got to the field I was running a few minutes late, which always drives me crazy.

I raced out of the car as Mom yelled, "Have a great game, baby!"

I joined the team on the field. "How is having a dog?" Riley asked.

I rolled my eyes. "Not easy," I said.

Coach Wendy called us in for a huddle. "Remember, girls," she said. "This is the first game, and we have a whole season ahead of us. Let's perform as a team. That's the goal today, not making goals."

I overheard the other coach yell in their huddle, "Do what you have to do to win!" I was really grateful right then for Coach Wendy.

The whistle blew and we were on. Isabella had a few really great runs, and Madeline and I passed down the field, but we couldn't seem to score. I noticed Riley was lagging behind.

"C'mon, Riley!" I said.

She looked really nervous.

Coach Wendy had taught us during drills to call out as we were about to pass. I got the ball and called to Madeline, who ran right next to me. We managed to get the ball down the field, but I was blocked. In practice we had a drill that we ran again and again where it was Madeline, then me, then Riley. I looked up and saw Riley was open, and I kicked to her.

Her face was surprised and she jumped a little, then kicked right over the ball and fell. The other team snatched the ball and went back up and scored

"It's okay, Riley!" I heard Coach Wendy call. "Get your game back on!"

"Sorry," Riley mumbled as she jogged past me.

We set up the same play again. Madeline, who just seemed to appear next to me, passed to me. Then I passed to Riley. She tripped again. I felt bad, but I was also getting a little frustrated.

"Time-out!" called Coach Wendy, and we ran to the huddle.

Riley looked down, not wanting to meet eyes with any of us.

Madeline threw her arm around her. "Riley, you can do this," she said. "This is just nerves!"

"Yes!" said Coach Wendy. "I need you to relax and trust yourself, Riley. You have a whole team behind you."

That didn't seem to help. On the next play Isabella passed to Riley, and she slipped.

I saw Coach run down the sidelines. "Riley!" she called. "You have this!!"

But at that point I wasn't taking any chances. I passed back to Madeline instead, and we took the ball down the field. Madeline passed back to me, and instead of passing to Riley, I ran down and sank it in the net.

Finally!

Madeline and I jumped up and down, giving each other high fives.

"Molly!" Coach called, and pointed.

I figured she was rotating Samantha in for me to give me a break. Instead she sat down next to me on the bench.

"I'm taking you out so you can get a little perspective," she said. "You left Riley out of that play, and that's not how we do things as a team. We work with each other, not around each other. Okay?"

The whistle blew and she jumped back up.

I was so surprised. I mean, I scored. I know we were supposed to work on teamwork, but I didn't just break away and score. Madeline worked the ball with me. Plus, I scored!

Ten minutes later Coach Wendy put me back in.

"What was that about?" asked Madeline.

"Teamwork," I said.

She looked puzzled, but the ball was in play again.

I passed to Madeline, who passed back to me. I looked up and saw Riley hovering and passed to her. She got the ball, but the other team snatched it and ran back up the field to score again.

I kept my head down and kept passing. Finally, on the fourth play Riley got the ball and ran with it. I was so surprised I kind of stood there for a second, then ran down behind her.

"You've got it, Riley!" called Madeline.

Sure enough, Riley scored. She let out this big whoop, and I gave her a high five. I was happy, but it was too late. We lost 8–2.

"Okay, girls," said Coach Wendy in the final huddle. "We didn't win in scoring, but we won in teamwork. Riley, I know you had a tough game, but your teammates didn't give up on you. Molly and Madeline kept running the play that we practiced so much. They did it again and again until you broke through and scored. That is true teamwork, and I am so proud of you girls!"

As we were shaking hands, I thought about what Coach Wendy had said. I kept passing because she told me to, but I didn't really think about Riley. She really did hang in there and kept trying. I felt bad for thinking about winning instead of thinking about how she felt.

I was disappointed about losing, but mostly I was disappointed with myself. Mom, Dad, Jenna, and Kelsey came down to the field, with Ruby barking and nipping at Jenna's heels. Rusty followed Dad.

"Are you keeping her?" asked Madeline, bending down to pet Ruby, who was chasing a leaf.

"No," said Mom. "We're just taking care of her until tomorrow."

"She is just too cute," said Isabella, making baby sounds at her.

Ruby ignored all of us and continued to chase the leaf.

I felt something wet on my hand and looked down to find Rusty's nose nuzzling it.

"Hi, boy," I said. He rubbed his head on my leg, kind of resting it there.

Dad had to chase Ruby down the field, which annoyed me. My feet hurt from the new cleats, and I just wanted to go home.

Finally, we got Ruby in the car. Rusty followed us into the back, and he sat down at my feet, looking up at me. I softly scratched him behind his ears.

I looked at him and he cocked his head, watching me, maybe realizing that I was a little unhappy. Then he put his head on my lap. Rusty wouldn't get mad if I missed a ball. He was a loyal friend.

We drove home like that, with him resting on me and me leaning on him a little. It hadn't been a great day, but I felt so much better that my new friend was looking out for me.

Chapter Thirteen
Mom Saves the Day

The next day I had to get up and work four hours at the Park, which was not good. I didn't mind working, but we'd had another sleepless night. Ruby was up for most of it howling at the moon, which was really bright that night.

"Harvest moon," Dad groaned as he and Mom ran around the house, trying to pull all the shades and curtains shut.

I think even Rusty was stressed out, because he had his paw over his eyes. I brought him up to my room, and he got all the way under the covers with me. It was nice to sleep with a soft dog. Especially one who actually slept and cuddled.

We all had to be at the restaurant at six thirty in

the morning. I was usually up early, but we had to drag Kelsey out of bed, and she was grumpy.

"At least you just need to stand behind the counter," Jenna told her. "If you were a waitress, you'd need to be running around. And Sunday mornings are the busiest."

"Busy is good for business," said Mom, almost automatically.

We all tumbled in at 6:25 and scrambled to get to our stations. Lindsay was waiting for Kelsey at Donut Dreams, and Lily and Rich were prepping the coffee trays. I jumped in.

To prep the coffee trays, you made sure all the sugar bowls were full, that the little milk and cream pitchers were full, and that you had extra spoons ready. People liked their coffee right away in the morning, so we were all working fast to make sure the waitstaff could just grab a tray and go.

Nans called us in to go over breakfast specials. The omelet of the day was a western omelet, which had peppers and ham. The pancake special was banana.

"And for dessert," said Nans, "our special of the day is a new donut, Molly's Apple Pie donut. It's a new recipe and one that I'm sure will be a hit."

I perked up.

"Molly gets a donut named after her?" asked Kelsey.

"She does," said Nans. "Because she came up with the idea."

"Hmmph! I'm jealous!" Jenna said jokingly and stomped out of the kitchen, pretending to be mad.

Everyone got a taste, and as Nans handed me mine, she winked. "The pie is perfect now," she whispered. "And I think these are almost there!"

I was still grumpy from losing the game and from not sleeping. I bit into the donut. I felt a little better immediately.

"Wow," I said to Nans. "I think I have a new favorite!"

"Coffee on table four, please," said Jenna, and I shoved the rest of the donut in my mouth, grabbed the pot, and headed over . . . right to Eric Sellers, his mom, and his older sister.

I could not believe my bad luck lately.

"Hi, Molly," Eric said.

"Hi, Eric," I mumbled, and poured coffee into his mom's cup.

As soon as it was full, I rushed straight back into the kitchen.

"What's wrong?" asked Jenna, passing me with a tray. "You look a little freaked out."

"Nothing," I said, and took a deep breath. I tried to avoid Eric's table after that.

Rich and Jenna didn't seem to notice, because it was really busy. But Kelsey did. She saw me from across the room and pointed to Eric's table, then made a face.

I shrugged and went back into the kitchen to hide.

"Hey, I need help," said Rich. "Syrup on four, please, Molly. Okay?"

"Got it," I said.

I grabbed a syrup pitcher and went to drop it at table four. You had to wipe down all the syrup pitchers after the breakfast rush because they got so gross and sticky.

As I turned from table four, I saw someone waving a hand at me. It was Eric's mom.

I could pretend I didn't see her and rush by, but I knew Grandpa would have a fit. I groaned inwardly and went over.

"Can I get you something?" I asked, trying to look only at her.

"Sweetie, I know you're busy, but I need some more milk for my coffee, please."

Eric was doodling on his place mat and didn't look up. His sister was watching me.

"Hey, aren't you Jenna's little sister?" she asked.

"I am," I said, starting to turn away.

"You're in Eric's class, right?"

"I am," I said.

I felt my stomach flip around again. I looked down and realized that Eric wasn't doodling on his place mat. He had his family tree sheet out, and he was writing on it.

"Let me get that milk for you!" I said, and turned and fled into the kitchen.

Mom had been working in the office after she brought us to the Park, and she came into the kitchen for another cup of coffee.

"Did you go through a whole pot already?" Grandpa joked. Mom drank a lot of coffee.

"We were up all night again with Ruby," Mom groaned.

I filled up the pitcher with milk but was just standing there. I really, really didn't want to deal with Eric Sellers.

Family Recipe

"What's wrong?" asked Mom, narrowing her eyes.

I sighed. You just could not get anything past her.

"Eric Sellers is at table four," I said. I held up the pitcher. "His mom needs more milk."

Mom looked at me for a second. "You know, Jenny Sellers and I grew up together. Give me the pitcher."

I handed her the pitcher. Grandpa looked like he was going to say something, but Mom shook her head and gave him a look.

"I've got this. It's been a while since my waitress days, but it's like riding a bike. Come on, Molly," she said, and strode out of the kitchen.

"At least put on an apron if you're going to serve!" yelped Grandpa.

Mom went right over to table four. "Jenny!" she said. "I haven't seen you in ages! How are you?"

"Melissa, it's so good to see you!" said Mrs. Sellers, standing up to give Mom a hug. "How have you been?"

"Can't complain," said Mom. "Are you still teaching at the community center?"

"Sure am," said Mrs. Sellers. "You know, I'll be stuck in preschool for the rest of my life!" She laughed heartily, and Eric looked a little embarrassed.

"I hear Eric is in Molly's history class," said Mrs. Sellers.

Eric looked startled.

"I hear that too," said Mom, putting her hand on my shoulder.

"Well, I don't know how you feel about this family tree project," said Mrs. Sellers. "But it's causing a lot of drama in our house."

"How so?" asked Mom.

"Well," said Mrs. Sellers, "you know Jeff and I divorced years ago."

"Yes, I did hear that, and I'm sorry," said Mom.

"Oh, no, no," said Mrs. Sellers. "It actually all worked out. I'm married now to Dan Ostfield. You remember him?"

"I do," said Mom. "He was a nice guy!"

"Yep, and he still is," said Mrs. Sellers. "I suppose at some point I may change my last name to Ostfield," Mrs. Sellers continued. "But Eric didn't like the idea of me having a different name than his, so I kept Sellers. For now anyway."

"I can understand that," Mom said.

"And Jeff is now married to Laura Farmer."

"Oh, Justin Farmer's sister!" said Mom.

"Right," said Mrs. Sellers. "We're all very happy and the kids are happy. But this family tree is a problem. Eric seems to think there's just a straight line in every family and the tree has an even number of branches, like Ms. Blueski drew on the worksheet. But our family has a few more branches."

"But that's not what the worksheet has on it," said Eric.

"Eric really wants to include Laura and Dan in our tree, because they're like a second mom and dad to him," said Mrs. Sellers. "And he has stepbrothers and stepsisters. But he's not sure how to do it, and he's embarrassed to have a tree that looks different from everyone else's."

"I see," said Mom, giving me a look.

"I told him to ask around, because I'm quite sure there are many kids in the class who have branches that weave around, but he claims no one does."

Ohhhh. So that's why Eric kept asking me about my "moms."

"Well," said Mom, looking at me.

"I have a couple different branches," I said.

Eric looked up.

"I was trying to figure out how to put my biological mother on there but have my mom in the main spot," I said. "Because, you know, Mom is my mom."

Eric nodded. "Yeah," he said. "I mean, Dan isn't my dad—my dad is my dad. But it doesn't feel right not to have Dan on the tree too."

"He's been putting off this project," said Mrs. Sellers, pointing to his worksheet.

"Me too," I said.

"I have an idea," said Mom. "Eric, can I see that sheet?"

Eric handed it to her.

"I can make a copy of this in the office. I don't know how much time you have, but Molly can take a break soon. Maybe we put you guys at a table with some donuts and you can help each other?"

Eric smiled, and I grinned back at him.

"That would be awesome," Eric said.

Mrs. Sellers beamed too. "Thank you, Melissa," she said. "That would be terrific. See, Eric?" she added, turning to her son. "I told you that if you asked, other people could help!"

"Okay," said Mom. "Molly, you can take a break

in twenty, which gives you, Eric, time to eat the rest of that breakfast!"

Eric picked up his fork and started hungrily eating his pancakes.

"Good, right?" asked Mom, and he nodded.

"Best in town!" said Mom. "See you around, Jenny!"

"Thanks again, Melissa!" said Mrs. Sellers. "You have no idea how relieved I am."

I smiled. She wasn't the only one.

Chapter Fourteen
It's Dog Day!

I was feeling so much better about things after we spoke to the Sellerses that I didn't mind that we were so busy. Sundays are always busy, but it seemed even more so today.

I cleared table five and noticed that the Sherers were seated at table two, the big round top.

"Warning," Jenna whispered, passing by. "Tornado on two! Can you make sure there are extra napkins?"

I breezed over with a stack of napkins.

Christopher jumped up. "Hi, Molly!" he said. "I get to have chocolate chip pancakes today because it's a Special Occasion!"

"Is it your birthday?" I asked.

He shook his head, but his face had a wide grin.

"No, it's Dog Day. Today, we're getting a doggy!"

"Oh, Christopher!" I said. "I am so jealous. I've wanted a dog my whole life!"

"You should ask your mommy and daddy for one," said Christopher.

"I have," I said. "And they keep saying no!"

"Were you bad?" Christopher asked in a whisper. "Because my brothers and I had to do chores and clean up to show our mom and dad that we can help take care of a dog."

"I have definitely done my chores and listened to my parents," I said, trying not to crack up. "But they say it's just too much work for us."

"It *is* a lot of work," said Mr. Sherer. "We are totally nuts for having three kids and getting a dog!"

"But we love dogs," said Mrs. Sherer. "And with the kids so young, we're home all the time. Plus, the dog will have three active children to keep her busy."

"And we're nuts," added Mr. Sherer.

I saw Jenna coming out of the kitchen with a full tray. I could tell she needed help.

"Hang on," I said, and grabbed the tray rest, which is this foldout thing that holds the tray while you unload all the plates.

"Thanks," said Jenna, putting the tray down and then setting the pancakes in front of the boys and eggs in front of Mr. and Mrs. Sherer. "Can I get you guys anything else?"

"Syrup!" yelled Christopher.

Mrs. Sherer gave him a look.

"Syrup, please," said Christopher.

I smiled. "Syrup coming right up!" I said.

"Molly is adopted," said Christopher.

"Christopher!" said Mrs. Sherer sharply. "Oh dear, Molly. I am so sorry."

"It's okay," I said. "I *am* adopted."

"Her mommy and daddy adopted her like we're going to adopt the puppy today."

"No, Christopher, not like a puppy!" said Mr. Sherer loudly. "For goodness' sake!"

"No, it's not the same," said Mrs. Sherer. "But let's try to help Christopher understand. When you adopt something or someone into your family, they or it becomes a part of your family. A sister is not the same as a puppy, but they're both members of your family and you love them very much."

"I'd like a puppy way more than a sister," said Christopher.

"Well, you are definitely not getting a sister," said Mrs. Sherer.

"Sisters are pretty awesome, though," said Jenna.

"I have enough brothers," said Christopher.

"Yes, you do," said Mr. and Mrs. Sherer together.

"Okay, Christopher, you enjoy those pancakes!" said Jenna. "Molly, I need you in the kitchen."

I got the syrup for the Sherers, dropped it off, and went to the kitchen.

"What?" Grandpa asked, looking up from where we stacked the tickets. He was watching to see what people were ordering and how long the orders were taking.

"Nothing," said Jenna. "Just some talk between girls."

She started filling up some glasses with orange juice at the counter on the other side of the kitchen, and I followed her. Nans was at the counter too, rolling out dough for the donuts.

"Are you okay?" Jenna asked me in a whisper. "I mean, Christopher is just a kid and all, but still . . ."

"Yeah," I said. "It just seems like suddenly the fact that I'm adopted is . . . I don't know."

"What happened?" asked Nans gently.

"Christopher asked if adopting Molly was like adopting a puppy," said Jenna. "Plus, there's been some stuff going on at school."

"Well, Melissa told me about the school stuff," said Nans, cutting round circles out of the dough.

I wasn't surprised. In our family we really do tell each other everything.

"I mean, I am adopted," I said. "It's a fact. That's how I got here. But it's not really a big issue."

"I understand that," said Nans. "And it isn't anything you should have to explain if you don't want to."

"Christopher's just a kid," said Jenna. "He doesn't know any better."

"That's right," said Nans. "He's curious and asking questions, which is natural. But it's still not okay if it makes you uncomfortable, Molly."

I thought for a second. "I'm not uncomfortable with it," I said. "That's the thing. But it seems like everyone else is uncomfortable with it and no one knows how to deal with it *but* me."

"Order up for table three!" came a voice from the kitchen.

"I have to pick this up," said Jenna. "I'll be back."

She looked at Nans, and Nans waved her off. Nans was taking donuts out of the fryer with a slotted spoon, and getting ready to put the next batch in. The donuts looked perfect when they came out, but once she put them on the rack to cool, the inside oozed out a little bit.

"That filling won't stay in," I said.

"I know," said Nans. "And it was driving me crazy not to have it perfect, just like my pies. But you know what?"

"What?" I asked, wondering if she was going to let us all eat the donuts that weren't perfect.

"It tastes good anyway. And this is a family recipe," said Nans. "Family is sometimes messy. And sometimes it's not so bad if what's inside comes out."

"Like our feelings?" I asked.

"Yes, feelings," said Nans. "Especially all the love we have on the inside."

She finished the batch and had about two dozen donuts on the rack. Most of them were kind of drippy.

"I think these are going to be a hit, Molly," said Nans. "And I think they're just perfect."

"I'm pretty sure I have a table with kids who would love these," I said.

"The Sherer kids?" laughed Nans. "They love anything with sugar!"

"You know," I said, "maybe on Sundays for the next month we can pass out donuts to all the tables for dessert, on the house. That way we can introduce people to new flavors they might not buy at first."

Nans smiled. "Hey, Jack!" she called to Grandpa. "Your granddaughter over here has your business sense. Just listen to this plan she has!"

I explained to Grandpa, who did a little excited hop and gave me a huge hug.

"That's brilliant!" he said. "Let me round up the Donut Dreams team to help!"

"It runs in the family!" said Nans, and then she threw a few more donuts into the fryer.

I skittered out to the floor because I realized I had been missing for a while. The Sherer table was a mess, and Jenna was trying to collect all the sticky napkins.

"I've got it," I said, coming up behind her.

She gave me a grateful look, then moved on to do coffee refills at her other tables.

The rest of the shift was pretty busy but not terrible. Grandpa handed Lindsay, Kelsey, and me each a big platter of the apple pie donuts with a set of

tongs. We went from table to table offering them—
and let me tell you, it went over extremely well.

People were so excited. We heard a lot of "Oh, I
shouldn't have a donut, but . . . ," and then they ate the
whole thing in three bites.

Chapter Fifteen
A New Member of the Family

After we were on donut duty, as Grandpa called it, Lindsay and Kelsey went back to the Donut Dreams counter, because Sunday was not only the busiest day for the Park, it was the busiest day for donuts.

Mom had made a space for us in her office so that Eric and I could tackle the family tree. I had the copy of Eric's tree Mom made for me. I tore a page out of my notebook and put a fresh piece of paper in front of me. Eric had his page with a tree template on it.

"Okay, so how are we going to do this?" I said, staring at my blank piece of paper.

"I've been thinking," said Eric. "Maybe we just have to be a little creative. Think outside the lines . . ."

I watched as he drew in more branches on his

sheet, some that were long, and some that were short.

"Now there are more spaces," he said.

I nodded. "You could also"—I grabbed a pencil and started drawing—"do this . . ." I drew more of a forest, with a bunch of trees.

"That might work better," said Eric.

"Right?" I said. "Because this way you can see how all the trees around you make up the forest where you live." I shrugged. "You can do your family tree however you like. This is just a suggestion."

"That's really smart, Molly," said Eric. "This way you can see that no tree really stands alone. It's . . . what's that word we learned in English lit where an image or an idea stands for something else?"

"Metaphor," I said. "It's a metaphor for the fact that no family is really alone, that it takes a lot of trees . . . a whole forest, really."

Eric nodded and continued sketching, and so did I. I filled in our family, then added a tree next to us with Aunt Miranda and Uncle Adam.

I sighed.

"What?" asked Eric. "Are you stuck?"

"Yeah," I said. "I mean, I guess my biological mom should be on here, but I don't know how to add her."

"How about a leaf, then?"

"A leaf?" I asked.

"Yeah, just a leaf. I mean, your biological mom doesn't play into your family, but she is a part of you, or I guess you're a part of her. So just one leaf on the big branch."

I thought about that. "Actually, that seems about right," I said.

I sketched in a leaf off to the side. Mom and Dad still sat on the big wide branch, and Jenna, Kelsey, and I were smaller branches off their big one.

"Hey, I think we figured it out!" I said, and I looked over at Eric's page. "Wow."

I had never realized he could really draw. There were all sorts of trees and bushes, and some of them touched or the branches crossed. Some had flowers. It was really beautiful.

He laughed. "I'm going to present this as My Tangled Tree Family Forest."

"But tangled is good here," I said.

"It works for me," said Eric. "I'm sorry that I was pestering you about your tree in class."

"It's okay," I said. "But you should have told me why."

"Yeah, I realize that now," he said. "My mom says that sometimes I don't think before I speak. My sister says I'm just annoying."

I stifled a giggle.

"I'm sorry if it came out the wrong way and I upset you," said Eric.

"Apology accepted," I said. "And thanks for that."

"Your mom ordered these for you two," said Nans, putting down a plate of apple pie donuts.

Eric's eyes got big.

"The perks of being in the family business," I said.

"These are called Molly's Apple Pie donuts," said Nans. She winked. "It's a special family recipe."

Eric inhaled the donut and said, with his mouth full, "I'd like to be a part of your family!"

I nodded and bit into mine. "Sweet, delicious, and a little messy," I said, wiping my fingers on a napkin and smiling at Nans. "Our family is perfect."

※　※　※　※　※

I was really glad to have the family tree project done, but I was still dreading the next thing we had to do: give Ruby back to Mrs. Rose.

Jenna, Kelsey, and I all left the restaurant with

145

Mom and drove to the park. Mrs. Rose had found a family who wanted to adopt Ruby, and they were meeting her at the park for the exchange.

We were meeting Dad, who was bringing the dogs from home. Our meeting spot was the gazebo near the baseball field, and we all quietly walked over.

"I know you're sad, Molly," said Mom. "But I'm not so sure it's a great time to have a puppy in the house."

"I know," I said. Even I had to admit this weekend proved she was right. Between being kept up all night and having Ruby demand constant attention and make messes, not to mention eat my cleats, it had been exhausting. "But I'll still miss her."

"We'll all miss Ruby," said Mom.

"No, we won't," said Kelsey. Mom gave her a look.

"What?" said Kelsey. "That dog is a pain. But I like Rusty."

So did I. I hoped Mrs. Rose would find a good home for Rusty, too.

We sat on the bench in the gazebo and watched for Dad, who was planning to run to the park with the dogs. He thought it would be a good idea for them to get some energy out before they went to a new home.

Then we saw Dad and Rusty come running up the path. Dad seemed to be holding Ruby.

"What happened?" asked Mom as he jogged up.

"Well, turns out the run was a little much for the puppy," said Dad, panting a little. "But Rusty here handled it like a champ." Rusty sat down next to Dad and looked up at him. "Good boy, Rusty!"

We all sat there, waiting. Rusty put his head on Dad's lap.

"Awww, such a sweet pup," said Jenna.

Ruby barked and barked. After a while I saw Mrs. Rose walking down the path, and Ruby went berserk barking and running around.

"Hello, dear," said Mrs. Rose, bending down to pet her. "You ready to meet your new family?"

Just then Christopher Sherer and his two brothers came tearing down the path, screaming, "Doggy Day! Doggy Day!"

Wait, Ruby was being adopted by . . . the Sherers? I remembered what Christopher had said at the Park, but I hadn't really put it together.

Mr. and Mrs. Sherer were trotting after the boys.

"Okay," said Mrs. Sherer. "Now, boys, we talked about this, right?"

The three boys stopped screaming. They sat down on the ground, crisscross applesauce style, and watched the dogs.

"Remember, a new puppy can get excited," said Mr. Sherer. "So we have to be very calm."

The boys nodded, not taking their eyes off Ruby.

"Ruby," said Mrs. Rose, squatting down, "meet your new family."

It was almost like Ruby understood, because she looked at the boys and went running over, wagging her tail. One by one she licked each boy's face as they laughed and tried to pet her. Then she stopped barking and curled up in Christopher's lap, resting her head on his knee.

"Well, will you look at that," said Dad.

"That looks like it was meant to be," said Mom, smiling.

Christopher was beaming. "This is my new puppy, Ruby!" he said proudly. "She's adopted."

Everyone looked at me.

"But it doesn't matter," said Christopher. "Because Mom says that it doesn't matter how you get your family. It just matters that you're a part of it."

I smiled. "That's exactly right, Christopher."

The boys were quietly taking turns petting Ruby, and she seemed to bask in the attention. It felt a little weird that she'd been such a handful for us but seemed right at home with the Sherers. But I couldn't be upset that she'd found the perfect family for her.

"Okay, slowly, gently," said Mr. Sherer.

The boys slowly got up. Ruby stood next to Christopher and looked up at him.

"Ready, Ruby?" asked Christopher.

Ruby barked, and Christopher looked delighted.

"Okay, gang," said Mrs. Sherer. "We are homeward bound!"

We all said goodbye to Ruby, even Kelsey, who petted her head and said, "I'm glad you will be loved. Just not by us."

We watched as the Sherers walked out of the park, with Ruby trotting calmly next to Christopher.

"Well, she didn't even look back, did she?" Mrs. Rose chuckled.

"That was a great match," said Dad.

"I have an eye for these things," said Mrs. Rose. "Okay, now for the next one."

We all looked at Rusty.

"Goodbye, Rusty," I said.

Jenna bent down and nuzzled him, and Kelsey stroked his back.

"If we ever get a dog, I hope it's one like you," said Kelsey.

"Welllll . . . ," said Dad. He looked at Mom.

"Getting a puppy isn't right for us," said Mom. "But an older dog like this is a good fit for our family. Rusty is about six, which isn't a puppy, but he still should have quite a few good years left in him."

"So," said Dad, "if you girls are willing, we can take Rusty home."

The three of us looked up.

"He's ours?" screeched Jenna.

"He's yours," said Mrs. Rose.

"We got a dog! We got a dog!" Kelsey was jumping up and down. Then she stopped. "Wait, do I have to clean up his poop?"

"You all have to take turns," said Dad. "That's part of the deal."

Kelsey grimaced but said, "Okay, good with the bad. I can do that."

"C'mon, boy," said Dad. "Let's go home."

We thanked Mrs. Rose and walked toward the car. I heard Mrs. Rose say she'd bring over the paperwork for Mom and Dad to sign next week. Mom and Dad were holding hands. Jenna was holding Rusty's leash, and he was walking in between us. Our family had just gone from the five of us to the six of us, and it felt just right.

"I think I know what the best part of everyone's day is going to be!" said Mom.

"I know what the worst part is going to be if I have to walk Rusty tonight," said Kelsey. Rusty looked at her. "You know I love you anyway," she said.

I thought about our family and the fact that it had just grown a bit. Our family was a little crazy, a little loud, and a little messy. But it was also filled with a lot of love, and it usually dripped out in the best way. You could say it was perfect.

Still Hungry?
Here's a taste of the fourth book in the

series, **A Donut for Your Thoughts!**

Chapter One
I am a Super Sub!

"Casey Peters to the rescue! Yasss!"

I hung up the phone and tossed it onto the bed, pumped the music up loud, and danced around my room.

I had nothing planned after school, so I was excited to get called in to work with my BFF Lindsay Cooper at her family's restaurant, which also happened to sell the most delicious donuts ever made.

Back in the day, Lindsay's grandparents Grandpa

and Nans Cooper opened the Park View Table, which was now a booming family business in Bellgrove. True to its name, it sat right across the street from and had a dashing view of, you guessed it, the park! Between Nan's finesse in the kitchen and Grandpa's tight ship on the floor, the Park was the only restaurant in town worth talking about, with its legit menu and flawless service.

Nans initially started the Donut Dreams counter in the Park to stack enough dough (so to speak!) to send Lindsay's dad, their oldest child, to the university of his dreams. Unlike his brother and sister who stayed close to home, Mike Cooper ended up going away to school in Chicago. There, he fell in love with Lindsay's mom, Amy, and traveled to Europe with her.

Amazingly, out of all the places they could have chosen to live in this whole wide world, they came right back to Bellgrove to throw down roots and have kids—Lindsay and her younger brother Skye. Lindsay's dad took over Donut Dreams and Lindsay's mom became an art teacher at Bellgrove Middle School until she died two years ago.

My mom says it was Amy Cooper's choice to settle here instead of some big city or foreign land.

Mom knows this because she and Lindsay's mom were the original BFFs.

They even ended up having Lindsay and me at the same time, literally. Lindsay and I first mingled cries in the hospital, since we were born one day apart. Our oldest photo together is with our moms in the hospital nursery. And the rest is history.

I guess Lindsay's mom actually preferred the charmed small-town life that Lindsay and others hope to escape. I totally understand why Lindsay wants out—going to school with the same kids since kindergarten, everyone in your business, that sort of thing. But small-town life also has its perks. Not only delectable donuts, but also this feeling of safety and being known by everyone you see.

The truth is, Donut Dreams is more than just a pretty name for a donut spot, where people drive for hours just to sink their teeth into the pillowy sweetness of a banana cream or elderberry jelly donut.

Without Nan's bright idea, Lindsay's parents would have never met in Chicago, which means my BFF wouldn't be my BFF, because Lindsay wouldn't even be a thing. And where oh where would I be without Lindsay Cooper?

I pranced over to my dresser and pulled out my yellow Donut Dreams T-shirt, which read THE DREAM TEAM. I felt honored to be the only non-family member who worked at the Park on days like today, when one of Lindsay's cousins caught the cold or had a big exam.

Most of Lindsay's aunts, uncles and cousins were employees at the restaurant. The only family member of hers who wasn't recruited to work at the restaurant was her brother Skye, who was nine.

Thankfully I keep my room pretty neat—except for the closet and under the bed, that is—so I wasn't tripping over stuff looking for my stretchy jeans when my mom popped into my room carrying a load of clean, rumpled laundry.

My mom is the assistant principal of Bellgrove Middle, where I just started going this year. Ever since she got her back-to-school hairdo, I admired how her reddish brown ringlets framed her perfect moon face.

"Casey, it sounds like New Year's Eve in here!" she was shouting. "What's going on?"

I lowered the music. "They need my help at Donut Dreams today," I said. "Is it okay if I work for a few hours, isn't it Mom? Pleeeease?"

I already knew what the answer would be. As long as I aced my schoolwork and kept my room somewhat tidy, any opportunity I had to be responsible was all right with Laurie Peters.

"I hope you'll always be this enthusiastic about work," Mom said with a laugh. "Go ahead and make some dollars . . . not calories!"

Mom knew me to a tee. Lindsay and I always managed to sneak in donuts when no one was looking.

"Yes!" I cheered, my mouth already watering.

Mom left my room and I went back to zipping around in search of my comfiest jeans to wear with the bright Donut Dreams shirt that made me feel like a superhero whenever I slipped it over my head.